The Ten Thousand Dollar Man stood in front of her.

Her Ten Thousand Dollar Man...at least for all intents and appearances.

A sexy smile tilted the corners of his mouth. "I'm heading home to the girls. Need a lift home?"

The girls. Liam was a good father, always putting his daughters first. She told him she had her car and bid him good-night.

She feared he'd shake her hand. Instead, he gathered her in his arms. The heat that sparked from the contact made her tingle.

"I'll call you so we can figure out this ten-thousand-dollar date." His breath was hot in her ear and she struggled not to melt.

When he walked away, he turned and gave her a smile.

A smile that told her she'd just bought herself a lot more than she'd bargained for....

* * *

Celebrations, Inc.: Let's get this party started!

D0050324

Dear Reader,

A while back, I ran across a quote about "family" not always being about blood, but about the people you want to be part of your life. The idea of a family formed by choice spawned the idea for *Celebration's Family,* the fifth of six books in the Celebrations, Inc., series. Dr. Liam Thayer believes true love only happens once in a lifetime. He had that love once. He believes he'll never know it or the true sense of traditional family again. Kate Macintyre would like to believe in true love and happily ever after, but she's never experienced anything remotely like it. When they discover they both come from broken families, the need to reestablish that family bond is one of the catalysts that makes them fall in love.

I hope you'll enjoy Liam and Kate's story. Please be sure to look for the final book in this series, *Celebration's Baby.* It will hit the shelves in April. I love to hear from readers. So please drop me a line at nrobardsthompson@yahoo.com.

Happy Valentine's Day,

Nancy Robards Thompson

Celebration's Family

―

Nancy Robards Thompson

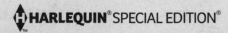
HARLEQUIN® SPECIAL EDITION®

If you purchased this book without a cover you should be aware that this book is stolen property. It was reported as "unsold and destroyed" to the publisher, and neither the author nor the publisher has received any payment for this "stripped book."

Recycling programs
for this product may
not exist in your area.

ISBN-13: 978-0-373-65797-1

CELEBRATION'S FAMILY

Copyright © 2014 by Nancy Robards Thompson

All rights reserved. Except for use in any review, the reproduction or utilization of this work in whole or in part in any form by any electronic, mechanical or other means, now known or hereafter invented, including xerography, photocopying and recording, or in any information storage or retrieval system, is forbidden without the written permission of the publisher, Harlequin Enterprises Limited, 225 Duncan Mill Road, Don Mills, Ontario M3B 3K9, Canada.

This is a work of fiction. Names, characters, places and incidents are either the product of the author's imagination or are used fictitiously, and any resemblance to actual persons, living or dead, business establishments, events or locales is entirely coincidental.

This edition published by arrangement with Harlequin Books S.A.

For questions and comments about the quality of this book, please contact us at CustomerService@Harlequin.com.

® and TM are trademarks of Harlequin Enterprises Limited or its corporate affiliates. Trademarks indicated with ® are registered in the United States Patent and Trademark Office, the Canadian Trade Marks Office and in other countries.

Printed in U.S.A.

NANCY ROBARDS THOMPSON

Award-winning author Nancy Robards Thompson is a sister, wife and mother who has lived the majority of her life south of the Mason-Dixon line. As the oldest sibling, she reveled in her ability to make her brother laugh at inappropriate moments, and she soon learned she could get away with it by proclaiming, "What? I wasn't doing anything." It's no wonder that upon graduating from college with a degree in journalism, she discovered that reporting "just the facts" bored her silly. Since she hung up her press pass to write novels full-time, critics have deemed her books "funny, smart and observant." She loves chocolate, champagne, cats and art (though not necessarily in that order). When she's not writing, she enjoys spending time with her family, reading, hiking and doing yoga.

This book is dedicated to Jennifer, who taught me the meaning of unconditional love.

Chapter One

A bachelor auction?

Really?

Dr. Liam Thayer waited for Cullen Dunlevy, Celebration Memorial's chief of staff, to crack a smile, or indicate he and the pretty blonde in the business suit at his side were delivering a bad joke to lighten up the impromptu staff meeting.

Please. He could use a little levity to jolt him out of his bad mood. It had been one of *those* mornings. The twins, Amanda and Calee, hadn't wanted to get out of bed. Five minutes before they were supposed to walk out the door, Amanda remembered that she was supposed to bring cupcakes for an after-school club meeting.

To spur the girls along, he'd said if they left on time, they could stop at the grocery store on the way. But then the dog got out, running several victory laps around the neighborhood, before Liam had been able to wrangle, harness and deliver him home.

They didn't have time to stop for cupcakes, and by the time he'd deposited the girls at Celebration Middle School, they were all out of sorts. Well, he and Amanda were. Not Calee, who lived in her own little world of sugar-plum fairies and nutcracker princes. As long as Calee was dancing, the world was a beautiful place. She was so much like her mother, who had also been a ballerina, before she'd given it all up to marry Liam and start a family.

He and Amanda, on the other hand, seemed to be cast from the same mold. This morning he'd left her with a promise that their housekeeper, Rosalinda, would leave a dozen cupcakes at the school's front desk in time for this afternoon's club meeting—which Amanda would have to cut short because she and her sister couldn't be late for their dance class.

Amanda had been dubious and a little surly. She hadn't wanted to go to dance class today.

"Why can't Rosie take Calee while I stay at the club meeting? Then Rosie can come back and get me. Or better yet, why can't I skip dance altogether?"

"Because you have a commitment, and Rosie doesn't need to be running herself ragged to accommodate you. She's already going out of her way to make sure you get the cupcakes."

It had only made matters worse when Liam had snapped, "Next time maybe you'll remember to tell me these things before we're walking out the door."

He shouldn't have said it. Not like that, dammit. Even if it was true and a lesson she needed to learn. Now, as he sat there in the conference room trying to change gears from dad mode to doctor, he couldn't get the image of Amanda's sad face out of his head.

At that moment he missed his wife, Joy, so much it almost leveled him. She'd always taken care of things like cupcakes, permission slips and new ballet shoes. She'd had an uncanny ability to almost read their daughters' minds or, on the off chance when they did end up in a bind—like they had this morning—she'd always been able to pull a rabbit out of her hat and make things work.

Liam didn't know how she'd managed it. She had been perfect like that. Tiny, intuitive and good-natured, Joy had always been all about her family.

A series of sickening flashbacks transported Liam to that night when the cop had stood on their front porch and asked, "Is this the residence of Joy Thayer?" He'd told Liam that there'd been an accident but wouldn't give him much information, just asked if he would come to the hospital. When he'd identified his wife's body, his life and the lives of their daughters had shattered into a million irreparable pieces.

Liam scrubbed a hand over his eyes, trying to erase the memory. It had been two years. When would life without Joy get easier? When would the numbness give way to the manageable ache that the grief counselor had promised would come in time? Maybe never. Because part of his soul had died right along with his wife that night. The part that lived and laughed and felt.

Now his daughters kept him going. Because life didn't stop to mourn. Hell, it didn't even slow down to regroup. It kept marching forward, and if you didn't get on your feet fast, it would drag you right along behind it.

He refocused, irritated that he had to waste time this morning listening to the chief and this woman rattle on about…bachelor auctions? For God's sake.

This had to be a joke.

But a sinking feeling warned him not to bank on Dunlevy delivering the punch line. Especially when his boss glanced over at the blonde and uncharacteristic warmth drew up the edges of his mouth.

"This is Kate Macintyre of the Macintyre Family Foundation," said Dunlevy. "She and her staff have been working tirelessly to raise money for the new pediatric surgical wing here at Celebration Memorial Hospital. I'll turn the meeting over to her and let her tell you more."

The new surgical wing—Joy had been excited about it. In fact she'd been one of the first volunteers to organize a kick-starter fund-raiser.

"Good morning," said the blonde.

What was her name again?

"Thank you, Dr. Dunlevy. I appreciate you letting me attend your meeting today. Even more, I am grateful that each of you has agreed to help raise money for the final leg of funding for this very special project. This pediatric wing is extremely near and dear to my family and me. I appreciate you all taking an active role in making it a reality."

Near and dear to her family? Liam glanced at her left hand. She wasn't wearing a wedding ring. Reflexively his thumb found the back of the band he still wore. It was the touchstone that kept him grounded, and reminded him of what was and always would be important in life. Family.

The blonde smiled at Liam's colleague, Charlie Benton, an internist, who was seated to her left. She held out a stack of pamphlets. "Would you mind taking one of these and passing them around, please?"

Eagerly Charlie obeyed.

Great. Judging by the look on his coworker's face, Liam would bet if she'd asked Charlie to run out to fetch her a bagel and a cappuccino, he would've fallen all over himself to oblige. Liam glanced around at the other men in the room. They all seemed transfixed, too. Apparently Liam was the only one immune to a pretty face and a great pair of legs.

"For the past three years, the Macintyre Family Foundation has partnered with the hospital to raise money to build a much-needed pediatric surgical wing," she said. "During this time we've been diligently working with the hospital's Department of Charitable Giving. They've been amazing. We only need five percent more to reach our two-million-dollar goal.

"That's why we were delighted when Dr. Dunlevy agreed to the idea of giving you all, the doctors of Celebration Memorial, the opportunity to play a key role in raising part of the remaining funds. When I learned that I'd be working with seven single male doctors, I thought, what was the chance of that?"

Her blue eyes sparkled as she looked from one face to the next, radiating enthusiasm and sincerity. She was doing a credible job.

"With seven eligible men, it only seemed natural to hold a bachelor auction. So, everyone, please save the date—one week from Saturday—for our first ever In Celebration of Bachelors auction."

Liam shifted in his seat, resisting the urge to excuse himself. This bachelor auction was not a joke, but there was no way in hell that he was going to subject himself to the humiliation of being sold off to the highest bidder. Even if the shenanigan would raise money for a good cause.

As a pediatric hospitalist and a single father to two teenagers, he didn't have enough time to devote to his daughters on a good day. He certainly didn't want to waste a night going out on a date with a woman who'd bid on him like a steer in a cattle sale. He might have been providing all the necessities, but he hadn't been able to give his children as much of himself as he wished he could. Not like his wife, who had always been there for them emotionally.

And, he had to admit, at the root of everything, participating in something like this felt disrespectful to Joy. Even if she was gone, it didn't mean he felt any less married. Certainly not single.

"Is something wrong, Dr. Thayer?" Cullen asked. "You look like you smell something."

Liam clicked his ink pen. He wanted to say, *There's nothing like the stench of a bad idea first thing in the morning.* But one glance at Kate Macintyre's hopeful expression—Kate Macintyre, that was her name—and he was weighing his words. "Is this bachelor auction idea a done deal? Do we have any other options?"

Kate blinked—once, twice—but her smile stayed unfalteringly in place. "Well, yes. I mean we're working on a very tight time line because of some special incentives, which I'll tell you about in a few moments." She glanced at Cullen as if for help.

"Yes, Liam, this is a done deal," Dunlevy said. "Is there a problem?"

"Yes. I have a family. I'm happy to make a donation, but I won't be participating."

With that, Kate's smile finally faltered. "Oh, I'm sorry. I thought Dr. Dunlevy said all members of the senior staff were single."

"We are," Cullen confirmed. Then he flashed Liam a look that was part warning, part *Let's not do this now* and mostly *Man up and be a team player.*

By this time the pamphlets had made their way around to Liam. He took one and passed the scant remainder to Austin Roberts, an emergency room doctor who was seated to Liam's left. The slick, glossy brochure featured a picture of a man, a woman, two kids and a yellow Lab frolicking on the green grass in the backyard of a nice suburban home.

The ideal family.

Liam waited to feel something—a stab, a pang or even a twist in his gut—but he didn't. He was numb. The only emotion coming through loud and clear was anger. He shifted his gaze to the bottom of the page, which was emblazoned with the Macintyre Family Foundation logo and the words *Family, Community and Education* written in bold red letters.

"It's true we're all single," Liam said. "I'm a widower."

"I'm sorry that you lost your wife."

Although her condolences seemed sincere, he shrugged, rejecting her pity and biting back the urge to say, *Can we just get on with this? I have things to do, patients to see.* Instead, he said, "A bachelor auction isn't a good fit. Maybe we can come up with something else."

"How can a date with a beautiful woman be a bad idea, Thayer?" asked Nick Chamberlin, who worked with Roberts in the emergency room.

Jake Lennox, the other staff internist, snickered. "It's a dirty job, but someone has to do it."

Liam glanced at his watch. "Knock yourselves out but don't count me in. I have patients to see. Is there anything else on the agenda?" He managed to close his mouth before he added, *Or is today's frat party over?*

"Yes, there's more, Dr. Thayer," Dunlevy growled at him. "We're talking about the bachelor auction first so that Ms. Macintyre can get back to her office. But while we're on that agenda item, I want to make it clear that we're a team. I expect every player to be on board."

Player. If that wasn't the operative word. Liam worked with a bunch of *players.* While he respected his colleagues as professionals, doctors who put heart and soul into serving the patients of this hospital, he and the six of them were worlds apart when it came to the time they spent away from work.

They were single.

He was a single father.

"Don't look so put upon, Thayer," ribbed Quinn Vogler, the new orthopedic hospitalist who'd recently joined the staff. "You're not the only single father in the bunch. I have a daughter, but I don't have a problem with this."

Right. Vogler had moved to Celebration from somewhere out west after a nasty divorce. Liam didn't know the details other than that Quinn had a daughter around Calee and Amanda's age who studied ballet at the same dance studio as his girls…or something like that. Liam wasn't sure. He didn't have time to keep track of his colleagues' personal lives.

"Out of all of us, it seems like you could use a night out," Vogler said. "You work too hard and take life way too seriously."

"Maybe you don't work hard enough, Dr. Vogler," Liam said.

Quinn scoffed, and Liam suddenly remembered his girls saying something about not liking Vogler's daughter very much because she was a bully. Liam hadn't put too much weight into that because he figured it had something to do with competition among teenage girls.

Now he wondered if the Vogler girl's needling nature came naturally. But Liam made it a policy not to meddle in his colleagues' personal lives. In turn he expected Vogler, the new guy, to show him the same courtesy.

Donning a layer of emotional armor, Liam crossed his arms over his chest and leaned back in his chair. Ignoring Quinn and silently challenging the others to test him further, he felt like the only grown-up in the room, embarrassed that this scene was unfolding in front of Kate Macintyre.

So he wasn't the only family man on the small staff. It didn't mean he needed or wanted a night out. The agonizing torture of those initial minutes, hours and days without Joy had accumulated into weeks, then added up to months that had stretched into years that were marked by the passing of birthdays, holidays and anniversaries that were nothing without her.

He did well to drag boxes of Christmas decorations down from the attic much less summon the energy to cajole the kids to put them on the tree. But somehow the three of them had managed to go through the motions. If their family had once been a tight circle when Joy was alive, now that she was gone, the circle was broken, and had become a straight line in which he and the girls were desperately hanging on to each other, grasping, making it through day by day.

Physically Liam left almost everything he had at the hospital. The emotional reserves were left for his kids. Not for a date with a woman who had won him in a sophomoric bachelor auction. Even if it was for a good cause, Amanda and Calee were the only company he wanted.

Kate Macintyre continued on with her spiel. "A moment ago I mentioned that this event would happen in short order because we have a special incentive." She paused, and, obviously knowing who her best audience was, she looked at Liam's colleagues with sparkling eyes, as if she were trying to contain her enthusiasm.

"Have you all heard of the reality television show *Catering to Dallas?* It stars Pepper Merriweather—who happens to be my sister-in-law—Sydney James, A.J. Sherwood-Antonelli and Caroline Coopersmith. It's filmed locally but is broadcast internationally. It chronicles the inner workings of the local catering company called Celebrations, Inc.

"It's a fun show, and it's really caught on with the television audience. They have a huge fan base. I just learned that a scheduled event canceled, and the producers have agreed to let us have the vacant spot. The bachelor auction will be recorded and broadcast at a later date on international television. They've also agreed to give viewers an opportunity to contribute to our cause at the end of the show. Even though the show will air later, the hospital's building fund will have an ongoing need."

Everyone except Liam broke out into a round of whooping fist bumps and applause.

Liam stood. "I'm sorry to be a wet blanket, but this isn't a good fit for me. I'll write you a check in lieu of participating. Just let me know what the average auctioned bachelor goes for these days, and I'll be happy to reimburse you for my part."

As he waited for her to quote him a figure, Kate gaped at him, the pleasant smile still affixed to her perfectly formed lips but uncertainty clouded her blue eyes.

"We've never done this before, so I'm not exactly sure." She paused for a moment, and he could see her virtually weighing her words. "I can assure you, Dr. Thayer, that the auction will be in very good taste. However, I certainly won't force you to do anything against your will."

Damn right, you won't.

But he had to give her credit. She was good. Tossing the ball back into his court like this, trying to make it hard for him to refuse. Too bad he wasn't playing, because once upon a long time ago she might have been just the type who could've changed his mind.

"I need to do my rounds now," he answered. "When you figure out how much I owe you, let me know, and I'll get you a check."

The chief of staff cleared his throat, and Liam's gaze zagged over to Cullen's impassive expression. The guy was only a couple years older than Liam, but the message in Cullen's eyes was full of authority, a promise that he wasn't going to cause a scene, but this match wasn't over. Cullen Dunlevy simply had too much class to duke it out in front of their guest and the rest of the senior staff.

Liam looked away, feeling like a jackass. But at least he'd stood his ground and won this set.

"I understand that you're busy," Kate said. "I appreciate your time this morning. How about if I call you, and we can set up a time to discuss this?"

She pulled a business card from her pocket and handed it to Liam. It read Kathryn Macintyre, President, Macintyre Family Foundation. He glanced at it, unsure how her giving him a card would help *her* call *him* as she'd offered.

Liam answered with a curt, noncommittal nod. "I don't have a business card on me right now. But you can reach me through the hospital."

With that, he left the conference room, closing the door after him. He'd made it only a few feet down the hall when a voice sounded behind him.

"Liam, hold on a moment."

He turned around to see Dunlevy standing outside the conference room, his hands on his hips.

The old familiar fight-or-flight sensation churned inside Liam, and he had to take a moment to reframe his urge to quarrel.

Reframe. That was the technique that the grief counselor had taught Liam when he felt like lashing out in anger. Of all the stages of grief, he seemed to fluctuate between feeling nothing—or as the counselor called it, "denial"—and wanting to lash out in anger. Or so thought the powers-that-be at the hospital who had forced him into counseling.

Those authorities had given him two choices: get help or take a sabbatical. Liam had still had enough of a handle on himself to know that he'd end up self-destructing if he had chosen the sabbatical. He couldn't be alone with himself for that long. Despite how he craved more time with the girls, they were so busy with school and their ballet program that he'd have way too much time on his hands. That wouldn't be good for the girls or his career.

Cullen Dunlevy had been one of the proponents of the ultimatum, and Liam still wasn't sure if he'd forgiven Cullen yet. As the chief of staff walked toward him, Liam knew that he'd better cool his jets or face the possible repercussions of Cullen pronouncing that the counseling wasn't working or that Liam wasn't trying hard enough.

But, damn him to hell, Cullen Dunlevy hadn't lost a wife; he wasn't left to raise two children and navigate alone the phase of his life when he and his high school sweetheart, his life partner, his *soul mate,* should've been dreaming of growing old together.

Damn Cullen Dunlevy. He'd never been married,

and he didn't have a clue what Liam was going through. Liam had to grind his molars to keep from spitting out his angry words at his boss.

Instead, he watched Cullen stand there with a disappointed scowl turning down the edges of his mouth, and his eyes darkened with... With what? Anger? Disappointment? Disgust? Liam felt like the wayward brother about to be set straight.

Dunlevy lowered his voice. "I know you've been through hell and back, but you have to get a hold of yourself. We've already had this talk, Liam."

"I understand," Liam countered in a monotone. "But my private life is private. My time away from the hospital is mine. I don't remember anything in my contract about fund-raising or bachelor auctions—"

"There is a clause in your contract that talks about performance bonuses. But if money doesn't motivate you, you know Joy would've wanted you to do this. She was one of the biggest proponents of the new pediatric wing."

Liam gritted his teeth harder. He had to keep from shouting or turning and punching a wall. Instead, he hissed the words in a low growl, "Dammit, Cullen, don't you dare go there. You leave Joy out of this. I said I'm happy to make a donation to the cause, and I think that's plenty."

"Do you?" asked Dunlevy. "You think that's plenty? Even though you are the senior staff member of pediatrics, the department that this fund-raiser is supporting? You don't think you should be there to represent it? I'm going to be there, putting myself on the auction block."

There was an edge to the chief of staff's voice, and Liam knew he was pushing it. But, damn Cullen to hell, he'd had the audacity to bring Joy's name into it. Because of that, Liam knew if he answered Cullen right now, Liam might come undone. Exactly how, he wasn't sure, but he didn't want to test the situation.

So he only tilted his head. "What is this? Peer pressure?"

Dunlevy heaved an exasperated sigh. "Look, I feel for you. We all feel for you. Losing Joy was…" He trailed off. His face softened, and he shook his head. "It was awful and unfair, but you can't keep being pissed off at the world. I need you to come back to the team."

Liam found his voice. "I haven't gone anywhere. I'm still here."

That *look* returned to the chief of staff's eyes. "You've been here in body but not in mind and spirit. Liam, before this happened, you were an opinion maker. The others have always looked up to you. They still do. I could really use your help with this project."

Project? "You mean farce?"

"Get off your high horse," Dunlevy said. "You know this is all in good fun. And, most important, it's for a great cause. We are seven single doctors. That alone is going to make headlines—we're going to be on television. This auction will draw every eligible socialite in the Dallas/Fort Worth area. They will bring their checkbooks to bid on bachelors who are doctors."

Liam knew it wouldn't do any good to argue that he didn't feel single. That his heart wasn't single. That he'd tried trusting a woman too soon after Joy's death and it had ended in disaster. But he knew the tactic the chief of staff would take. Cullen wasn't asking any of them to get married or even take this bachelor auction debacle seriously. It was one night—well, two, if you counted the night of public humiliation and the ensuing date.

"I'm going to lay it out plain and simple," said Dunlevy. "You're the most senior staff member after me. I'm not going to force you into this, but I'll say it again—I really could use your help."

The words hung in the air between them, an unspoken ultimatum.

Finally the chief of staff shrugged. "You think about it, Liam. Let me know when you've decided to be part of this team again."

Chapter Two

Joy Thayer.

Holy cow. It all made sense now, Kate thought as she stood in the empty break room of the Macintyre Family Foundation offices. She wrapped her hands around a mug of steaming-hot tea, letting the comforting warmth seep into her fingers and melt away some of the morning's stress.

Joy Thayer was Liam Thayer's late wife.

No wonder he was bereft.

After the meeting, as she had been waiting for the elevator, she'd glimpsed a memorial plaque that was displayed alongside the pictures of the hospital's board of trustees. She'd put two and two together as she was leaving the hospital, and had been haunted by the revelation ever since.

As much as she'd prepared for the presentation to the hospital's senior staff members, she hadn't planned on hitting a land mine like Liam Thayer. She wished that Dr. Dunlevy had informed her that she had a widower in the bunch—and not just any widower, *Joy Thayer's* widower—before she'd so exuberantly rolled out the bachelor auction plan at the meeting.

Dr. Thayer had obviously still not come to terms with his wife's death. Not that one ever fully recovered from something like that. Kate had experienced enough tragedy in her own life to understand.

Even though she'd only met Joy Thayer once—when the woman had single-handedly organized a fashion show luncheon to benefit the pediatric surgical wing early in the process—Kate had been touched by Joy's untimely death. The entire population of the Dallas metropolitan area had gone into mourning.

Joy Thayer was the type of charismatic good soul that everyone wanted to know and loved instantly. She radiated warmth and charm. And, as if all that niceness and class weren't enough, she had been gorgeous. One of the elements that Kate remembered best about Joy—besides her petite stature and fine-boned features—was the riot of strawberry-blond curls that hung halfway down her back. She had an effortless beauty that seemed to radiate from the inside out.

Now that Kate had had a chance to digest the situation, she wasn't surprised that Joy had been married to a handsome guy like Liam. They had probably made the perfect couple: good-looking, well-off, well connected, popular. His disposition left a lot to be desired, but he'd suffered a rough time in the grips of that profound loss.

Kate swirled the English Breakfast tea bag in her mug, then tossed it into the trash can. How long had Joy been gone now? At least a couple years. But even though Kate's encounter with the woman had been brief, Kate had a hunch that one didn't easily get over Joy Thayer and move on.

For that reason she would cut Liam some slack, even though his boss was being hard-nosed about it.

As she made her way back to her office, she pondered how she could shift the fund-raiser to make Liam more comfortable. She didn't want to turn down the publicity opportunity that being on *Catering to Dallas* would afford. And that hinged on the bachelor auction, which would be a good visual for television. Reaching that broad of an audience, they were bound to get generous donations from the television fans. Plus the other six bachelors seemed jazzed and ready to run with it. Before she'd left the meeting, some were even tossing about ideas for date packages and where they could take the lucky ladies who won them.

She couldn't think of a better way to make a dent in the remaining one hundred thousand dollars that she still needed to raise. Maybe it was for lack of a better idea—or maybe because *six* of the seven single, handsome doctors were ready and willing to auction themselves off—but they had to proceed with the auction with or without Liam.

She knew it was the right move, the prudent business decision, but she wasn't completely at peace with it.

She closed her office door and sank into her leather desk chair. Moving her mouse to activate her computer, she stared at the dark screen until the machine woke up from its nap.

I'm a widower with two teenage daughters.

Liam's words had echoed in the recesses of her mind all the way back to the office. If it were up to her, he would get a free pass. But she knew his boss wouldn't be keen on that thought.

After Liam had dashed off, Dr. Dunlevy had told her not to count Liam Thayer out. Whether that meant she should just count on the promised donation or his participation in the auction was still to be determined.

Yet Liam had taken her card and had given her the green light to call him at the office.

She would do that and pave the way. She just needed to come up with a plan that made everyone happy.

At twenty-nine, Kate had never been married. But she'd watched her own father sink into a dark funk after her mother had died. It was a depression from which he'd never fully recovered. Kate and her brother, Rob, had felt responsible for their dad. It had been a sad time in their lives, but they'd gotten through it together.

Dr. Thayer and Joy must have married young if his kids were teenagers. Yet he didn't appear to be much older than Kate was.

Kate's baby would've been five later this year if it had survived. It was a memory she'd tried to suppress since the topic of death and kids had come up this morning.

Actually she hadn't been able to get it out of her mind, despite the way she'd tried to ignore the dull ache in her heart. All the more reason to find a viable way out of this plan for the good doctor. One that didn't involve dates or leaving his kids at home.

She clicked on her email account, glanced at the full in-box, but she couldn't bring herself to open any of the correspondence. She swiveled her chair toward the floor-to-ceiling windows, stared out at the Dallas skyline and let her mind wander far away from the memory of the child she'd lost.

Bachelor auctions. Think. Fund-raisers. Think harder.

Cullen Dunlevy hadn't been thrilled with Liam's

steadfast refusal. So completely letting him off the hook seemed out of the question. And Dunlevy hadn't seemed pacified by Liam's offer to simply write a check. He wanted Liam to take an active role like his colleagues. She wasn't sure why Dr. Dunlevy was so adamant about Liam participating, but she'd definitely observed some underlying tension.

It didn't really matter.

Well, it shouldn't anyway.

But it did. To her.

If someone as busy as Liam Thayer didn't have the time—or the inclination—to auction himself off and go on a date, why was Dunlevy pressuring him? More important, what else could *she* come up with to make both men happy?

Emceeing wasn't an option because Maya LeBlanc, international chocolatier and supposed matchmaker, was fulfilling that role. But what to do with Liam?

Too bad he was so adamant about not being in the auction. I would've bid on him, she mused as she meditated on the geodesic sphere atop Reunion Tower.

Suddenly she had a thought; something that just might get Dr. Thayer off the hook, if he was willing to be a good sport and play along.

She glanced at the time on the lower right-hand side of her computer. Since it was close to six o'clock, he was probably gone for the day, and she wouldn't be able to reach him at the hospital. That was all right; it would give her some time to stew on the idea and make sure it was airtight. She'd give him a call tomorrow and see just how willing he was to put his money to good use.

Liam wholeheartedly supported the pediatric surgical wing—after all, the venture had been a project Joy was passionate about. But why did they have to do this asinine auction that would dishonor Joy's memory, embarrass his daughters and make a mockery out of the loss and grief he'd suffered?

He wheeled the car into the driveway and glanced at the glowing dashboard clock. It was nearly eight o'clock; darkness was creeping in and spreading over the sky like a stain. He'd stayed at the hospital making his final rounds later than usual. It was times like these that made him grateful he had dependable Rosalinda. Nanny, housekeeper and cook extraordinaire.

His stomach rumbled at the thought of the food Rosie would have waiting, hot and ready for him when he walked in the door. At this hour the girls would've already eaten. He hated missing meals with them.

Rosalinda had picked them up at the ballet studio after their dance classes and had fed them. At least he could rest assured that they were in good hands with her. She was a kind, trustworthy woman. Someone with a benevolent heart and no ulterior motives.

As he pressed the garage door opener, his gaze slid to the rearview mirror where he had a perfect view of the yellow two-story house across the street. Kimela Herring's house. Ever since letting Kimela get too involved with his family right after Joy had died, he was cautious when he left the house. Now he and Kimela mostly avoided each other.

He might have felt bad about having to set Kimela straight, except that she had broken a cardinal rule: she'd tried to use his daughters to get to him. What was worse, it had soon become clear that Kimela's objective was to send the girls away so that the two of them could make a life together.

The stupid thing was that Liam hadn't even seen

it coming. He'd been so out of it after losing Joy that Kimela Herring had nearly rearranged his household before he'd figured out what she was up to, all in the name of being a good neighbor.

That wasn't going to happen again. No way in hell. Calee and Amanda were thirteen years old. In five years they would be in college. In the meantime, the best thing he could do was to spend these years focusing on the girls and his patients.

He steered the car into the garage, pressed the button again, and watched the door moan and growl as it closed, eclipsing Kimela Herring's house.

And his emotions froze up again. The initial anger had evaporated, leaving him feeling zilch. Nada.

Nothing.

Except for an underlying fierce protectiveness that nothing was going to hurt his girls any more than they'd already been hurt. If anyone tried, he would take them out. And he didn't mean out on a date.

The thought had his mind skittering back to Kate Macintyre, and her offer to talk to him and help work out something. He sensed that she wasn't the type to strong-arm him into participating. That was decent of her. More than decent, he thought as he let himself out of the car. But she'd get his donation for the surgical wing. Wasn't the bottom line always what people were after?

She was obviously passionate about her job with her family's foundation. It was refreshing to meet a woman who was interested in the greater good of the community rather than feathering her own nest like his manipulative neighbor.

As Liam opened the door leading into the kitchen, their mixed breed dog, Frank, barked a greeting and the aroma of something delicious welcomed him home. The smells made his mouth water.

"*Hola,* Dr. Thayer," Rosalinda said. "Did you have a good day?"

He petted Frank. "Hi, Rosie. It was a tough day, but everything turned out okay. It's good to be home. Thanks for staying. I'm sorry I'm so late. Where are the girls?"

The grandmotherly woman took a plate from the cabinet. "They are upstairs showering and then they will do their homework. It's no problem to stay a little later. I'm happy to help you when I can. Are you hungry?"

"Rosie, you read my mind. Plus the smell of your delicious cooking could make anyone hungry. What's for dinner?"

By the time Liam had washed his hands, grabbed his e-tablet and sat down at the table, Rosalinda had set a plate of homemade meat loaf, mashed potatoes and steamed green beans in front of him.

"Thanks, Rosie," he said. "This looks delicious."

"You're welcome, Dr. Thayer. I hope you enjoy it. I want you to know I made the cupcakes and left them for Amanda at school. She was very sweet. Hugged me and thanked me when I picked her up from her dancing lesson. You have a darling girl with a good heart. Two sweet girls, because Calee, she is a good girl, too."

He was relieved that Amanda had thanked Rosie, especially when the generous woman had taken the time to make the treats from scratch rather than stopping by the bakery and buying them ready-made. Since losing her mother, Amanda, who had always been the more reserved of his twins, could sometimes appear sullen and aloof.

Liam had expressed his concerns about this to their

grief counselor, but the shrink had assured him Amanda was okay. He'd attributed her moodiness to typical teenage hormones compounded by the loss of her mother. Amanda was doing well in school and engaging in dance. The counselor had told Liam those signs made him believe everything would be fine. If she appeared to worsen or withdraw, Liam should let the counselor know.

Liam had found that the best way for all of them to cope was to stay as busy as possible. He had the hospital; the girls had school and dance. It seemed to be working since they all put in full days and came home so tired at night that they usually ate dinner, showered and fell into bed. They would get through this together. The best way was to just keep marching ahead.

"Rosie, what would we do without you?"

The woman laughed. "Well, you must try for the rest of tonight because I am going to leave now. Maria has to cover part of another shift tonight and has to go in a little early. May I get you something else before I leave?"

Rosie's family was small, consisting only of her daughter, Maria, and her infant grandson, Joaquin. Maria's boyfriend had left before the baby was born and hadn't been in the picture since. Now Maria lived with her mother, who kept the baby while Maria worked as the night manager at the Magnolia Hotel in downtown Celebration.

"No, thank you. You go home to your family and enjoy the rest of your night. I'll see you tomorrow."

Liam tucked into his dinner, focusing solely on feeding himself until he'd taken the edge off his ravenous hunger. Then he took a long, slow drink of iced sweet tea and flipped back the cover of his e-tablet. His curiosity had him searching the web for Kate Macintyre, wanting to know more about the woman and her family's foundation. He clicked on the first of several listings, an article about Macintyre Enterprises in the local weekly paper, the *Dallas Journal of Business and Development*.

It suddenly sank in that Kate Macintyre was part of *that* Macintyre family. The Macintyre oil family. He wasn't sure what he'd envisioned when he thought of Kate in her natural habitat, but the vague picture he'd formed in his mind's eye hadn't included *big oil*.

But then he read on, and discovered that Kate and her brother, Rob Macintyre, hadn't been raised with the silver spoon. Apparently they'd both worked hard to pull themselves out of the poverty of their youth. But her brother was the one who had amassed the fortune.

Another article mentioned that an accident had killed Rob and Kate's father, and nearly claimed the life of Rob's young son; this was the impetus behind the new pediatric surgical wing.

The boy had been airlifted to a children's hospital in Dallas, taking precious time that could've cost the boy his life. The Macintyres wanted to ensure that nothing like that ever happened to another local family, and so they had begun raising the funds for the new wing.

Liam realized how oblivious he could be when it came to matters outside his bubble. He knew the expansion was in the works, but until now, he had no clue of the story behind it. It made him appreciate Kate's efforts all the more.

It also made him feel woefully inadequate when it came to what was happening in the community. Joy had always kept track of things like that. She'd advise him on what was going on, and help him remember names and keep people straight so that he didn't embarrass himself.

He could virtually hear Joy say, *That's Kate Macintyre. Her brother, Rob, founded Macintyre Enterprises. Together the two of them founded the Macintyre Family Foundation. That's Rob's wife, Pepper, who once was the heir to the Texas Star empire before it crumbled. They were all key players in the community.*

So did that make Kate a socialite? She didn't act like one. She seemed too grounded and humble. Maybe one had to be born into social royalty. See, yet more proof that he was better off staying in his bubble. It reminded him of the saying, "If you have to ask, you can't afford it." But the more appropriate reconfiguration for his situation was "If you have to ask, you don't belong."

All that who's-who and what's-what made his head hurt. He hadn't had the time or the inclination for it when Joy was alive, and he had even less interest now, because he had his hands full with the things that were really important, such as his daughters and his job, which reminded him...

He typed the name of the auction, In Celebration of Bachelors, into the search engine. A webpage advertising the event came up. Charlie Benton, Quinn Vogler and Jake Lennox already had photos posted alongside descriptions of their proffered "dream dates."

Liam chuckled. What a bunch of dogs. It was a classic example of Pavlov's theory: the minute anyone said *women,* these guys started drooling.

Charlie's date was nicknamed The 007.

"You will dress to the nines in a gown you purchase on a predate shopping trip paid by Benton, Charles Benton. I will pick you up in an Aston Martin DB5 just like James Bond used to drive, and whisk you away to a supersecret location where we'll enjoy martinis—shaken, not stirred—as we watch the sunset."

He went on to describe dinner and dancing laced with a little bit of imagined danger, something about seduction and a whole lot of corny.

What the hell was Benton talking about?

Danger and *seduction.* Were they allowed to sell seduction as part of a prize package? Maybe that's where the danger came in—Benton pretending to be James Bond. The woman might crack a rib laughing.

Liam took another bite of meat loaf and read the other descriptions.

Vogler's entry was entitled A Red-Carpet Evening and featured a limousine, champagne, dinner and a movie.

It sounded like a nice evening, except for the fact that Vogler had to come along on the date.

A date with Lennox came with a promise in its headline: We'll Always Have Paris.

I'll be damned. Liam paused, fork midair. Jake was flying the winner to France for a night at the Ritz and dinner at Le Jules Verne, the restaurant atop the Eiffel Tower.

Show-off.

Liam snickered and shook his head. He wished there was a place to comment so that he could give unsuspecting ladies the heads-up on these guys. His snark was all in good fun. In fairness, he had to admit that his colleagues were good guys. Even if they did spend too much time at the hospital and on the golf course, and too little time on what really mattered in life.

And what was that? What really mattered? One size did not necessarily fit all when it came to answering those questions.

For Liam, it was family. His girls. Protecting them from more of life's hurts.

Okay, so six of his seven colleagues were unencumbered. Vogler was the only other one who had a child. That's probably why he was staying in town for the date and trying so hard to disguise a night out to the movies as some gala affair.

Liam tried to ignore the little voice that nagged him. *At least these guys know how to have fun. At least they are willing to donate their time in the name of something good.*

But Liam couldn't help but wonder why they just didn't donate the money they were going to spend on the flights to Paris and the shopping sprees and limousines.

As Liam was making a mental note to ask Kate that very question, his daughters raced into the dining room.

Liam stabbed at the tablet's off button, but only managed to switch pages rather than power down.

"Daddy!" squealed Calee. She threw her arms around his neck. Amanda hung back a little. As he hugged exuberant Calee, he could see Amanda over her sister's shoulder. The girl looked as if she'd grown again. She had a good four inches on tiny Calee, who had inherited her mother's petite stature. Amanda had gotten his height and bigger frame. The girl wasn't overweight by any means; she was just stockier and larger-boned than her sister.

They were starting to really look like the fraternal twins they were.

After Calee stepped back, Amanda hugged him.

He loved the way that each of his daughters was her own person, especially since they were twins. Vastly different, yet fiercely protective of each other.

Both girls wore their pajamas and had wet hair from

their showers. They smelled of the fruity shampoo and bath products they'd conned him into buying them when they'd dragged him to the mall a couple weekends ago. He breathed in deeply, savoring the scent of his little girls, just about the only fragrance in the world that soothed his weary soul. Mingling with Rosie's cooking, it was the smell of home.

The girls had been at school until two-thirty, and then, after Amanda's club meeting, they'd gone to the dance studio and were in classes until Rosalinda had picked them up at seven-fifteen. Despite the long day, they seemed to have more energy than he did after a good night's rest. A case in point that youth was wasted on the young. Well, maybe not wasted, but there was definitely an unfair distribution.

"Oh-em-gee," Calee said. Lately, she'd taken to speaking in what Liam called "alphabet soup"— acronyms rather than words. It seemed to be the trend among today's youth. "Are you going to be in that bachelor auction? Everyone's talking about it."

"What?" *Ugh.* Had she seen the website on the tablet before he'd exited the page?

"What auction?" he asked, borrowing a sly play from her book, one that he liked to call the "don't offer any more than is absolutely necessary" tactic.

Calee reached out and, with a couple confident taps, she pulled up the page he'd tried to hide as she and her sister had burst into the room.

"Duh. *This* auction. You were just looking at it. Oh-em-gee. Why are you pretending you weren't?"

She put her hands on her slim hips and affected a disapproving look. That was the thing about teenage girls: nothing got by them. That's why he was so careful not to do anything that might embarrass them or undermine the strict house rules under which he was raising them. Honesty was at the top of the list, and since he led by example, this was the perfect time to be truthful, a good teaching moment.

"I was looking at the website because I went to a meeting today, and they were talking about it. Some of my colleagues are going to be in it to help raise money for the pediatric surgical wing."

Did partial truth count? His colleagues were going to help. He'd just omitted the part about *him* declining to take part, too.

"I left to do rounds before the meeting was over. So I was checking the webpage to see what it was all about."

Amanda moved closer to stand beside her sister. She watched as Calee held up her hands. "Wait. Wait. Wait. You said your *colleagues* are doing it? Why aren't *you?*"

Liam was about to reassure her that he wasn't doing it because he didn't want to embarrass her and Amanda, but he was relieved when she didn't wait for him to answer.

"Oh-em-gee. You totally have to do it. You. Have. To. Do. It. Tonight at dance class Lacy Vogler was bragging about how her dad got *invited* to do it because she said he's the hottest dad in Celebration."

Lacy Vogler? She had to be Quinn's daughter.

"But I told her that he wasn't the hottest dad, that *you* were. Because you're his boss, right? *Right?*"

She was talking a mile a minute, and Liam was doing his best to follow what she was saying. Did this mean she *wanted* him to do the auction? He had a sinking feeling she might.

"Well, no. I'm not exactly his boss. He works at the hospital just like I do. I'm in charge of pediatrics, and he's in charge of orthopedics—"

"But you've been there longer, right? *Right?* Lacy Vogler just moved here, and we've always been here, and she's coming in and trying to take over. Please tell me you're going to do the auction, because if you don't, she will think she won and that her dad is better than you and—"

This time Liam held up his hands. "Whoa, Calee, take a breath."

He gave his head a quick shake, trying to stop it from spinning thanks to her breathless tirade. Also because he didn't like this trend of one-upmanship he was witnessing in her. And this wasn't the first time, either.

"Calee, in this family, we don't worry about keeping up with the Joneses. So it doesn't matter what Lacy says. The auction isn't to decide who has the hottest dad." He cringed before the sentence was completely out of his mouth. "Or however you put it."

Hottest dad? Since when did teenage girls even think about dads in those terms?

The way his daughter was reacting was exactly why he didn't want to participate in the auction in the first place. Well, okay, not *exactly* the reason. Sort of the flip side of the coin. Life and happiness weren't about looks, or who got the most bids or raised the most money.

"This auction is about helping. It's about doing something for the greater good of the community."

"Right, but Lacy's last name is Vogler? Not Jones?" Calee said. She'd also developed a habit of putting verbal question marks at the end of statements when she was trying to make a point.

When Liam squinted at her, she explained, "Haha, Dad. You said we're not interested in keeping up with the *Joneses*. It's Lacy Vogler, not Lacy Jones."

She spat the girl's name, as if the mere mention of it

left a bad aftertaste, and that bothered him, too. Maybe even more than the thought of putting himself up for auction.

"I know what her name is," Liam said. "You know what that expression means. Stop being a smarty-pants."

"So, then, that means you'll do it?" Calee said.

Had she not heard a single word he'd said? He glanced at Amanda, who was still conspicuously quiet. Probably because she couldn't get a word in edgewise when her sister was on a roll. Or possibly because she understood the implications of what her sister was trying to do.

Liam shrugged. "I don't know if I'll be in the auction. I will definitely contribute money, because the funding is what's important. The community and the hospital gravely need a pediatric surgical wing. It's a great cause, and I do want to help, but I'll have to think about whether or not I want to be in the auction.

"You see, the way it works is the women bid on the men. That money goes to the hospital. But then the guys have to take out the women who placed the winning bids on a fancy date and spend a lot of money. I think I'd rather give that money to the hospital. Instead of spending it on a date. Don't you think that's better?"

He paused to let the reality of that sink in. He wondered if Calee had been so caught up in outdoing Quinn Vogler's daughter that she hadn't even realized that being in the auction meant that a woman who was not her mother would expect to go out on a date with him.

He paused, waiting for the implications to sink in.

But Calee and Amanda were standing there staring at him, not giving him the horrified reaction he'd expected.

"Because you do realize that, by being in the auction, I would have to go out on a date?"

"It's not like you'd be cheating on mom or anything."

The voice came from behind Calee. Liam's gaze shifted to Amanda. She may have been the quieter of the two, but sometimes she seemed ages wiser. In fact, Joy used to call Amanda her "old soul."

"Well, no, I suppose not," Liam answered, feeling as if the last of his reasons for not participating in the auction were flying out the window fast.

"I guess I've been worried about how you two would feel if I took another woman out on a date. I didn't want to commit to the auction because I was afraid it would upset you."

Calee and Amanda looked at each other. Despite the fact that they were as different as night and day, they were as close as close could be. They stuck together. Calee, the more assertive of the two, always looked out for her sister and usually spoke for her, as well. Every so often the girls might get into a tiff, but no one besides the two of them got away with saying a cross word about the other without suffering the consequences.

Sometimes, like now, it was as if they had a secret, silent language in which only they communicated. It was almost telepathic. Liam saw them at work now.

"Dad," said Amanda, who had apparently been elected spokesperson for the matter at hand. "Just because some woman bids on you in an auction and you take her out, doesn't mean you have to like her. You know, you don't have to *like* her, like her."

Those matter-of-fact words, which weren't snotty or hateful, just truthful, were the well-placed punch in the gut he thought he'd avoided earlier when they had first started talking about the damn auction and the possibility of him spending time with someone who was not Joy. Only these words landed a little harder because now he felt foolish.

"Well, of course not," he said.

"But you wouldn't have to kiss her or marry her or anything like that," said Calee.

"So you're telling me that you two *want* me to participate?" Liam asked.

"Yes!" Calee cheered. Then she grew uncharacteristically serious. "Just as long as you don't let Mrs. Herring win you."

Chapter Three

Liam was early for the lunch meeting with Kate. She had called first thing that morning and said she'd come up with a plan to get him off the hook with Dunlevy. She wanted to discuss it with him.

A plan, huh?

Yes. One she'd rather not talk about over the phone. Or so she'd said and asked if they could meet for lunch. His first inclination, as he stood at the nurses' station, had been to decline and tell her that he'd decided to go through with the auction, but then he decided it couldn't hurt to hear what Kate had to say.

Now, as he waited alone at the table for two in Luigi's Italian Kitchen in downtown Celebration, he glanced at his watch. Eleven fifty-five. It was good to have a few minutes to take a deep breath. The morning had been hell. No different from any other day, except that he'd been forced to find a stopping place in the middle of his rounds. Usually he didn't take a lunch break; he'd grab something in between patients or meetings. It was strange to find himself outside the hospital walls at this time of day.

If Kate could offer a viable option other than the auction, he wanted to hear about it before he tipped his hand.

As he took a sip of the water the server had set in front of him, he glimpsed Kate entering the restaurant and stepping up to the hostess stand. Liam stood and waved. She said something to the hostess and then flashed a smile at him as she began walking toward their table.

He was warmed by the kindness she exuded, in spite of the fact that he'd acted like such a jackass in the meeting yesterday. Then again, she was a smart woman and probably realized it was her job to court anyone and everyone who could further her cause. The old saying about catching more flies with honey than vinegar came to mind. However, Kate seemed to radiate something more genuine than a person who was simply out to market her business purposes.

"Dr. Thayer," she said, extending her hand. "Thanks so much for agreeing to meet me on such short notice."

He nodded. "Please call me Liam." He pulled out her chair and helped her settle herself before reclaiming his own seat across the table from her.

"Actually I was glad you called," he said.

Her blue eyes widened, an unspoken question.

"I feel I owe you an apology. I didn't mean to be so difficult in the staff meeting yesterday. It was a tough morning, and your bachelor auction caught me by surprise."

She waved away his words. "No apology needed.

After I stepped back from the situation, I realized one size doesn't necessarily fit all when it comes to projects like this."

The server appeared and introduced himself. His eyes softened when he looked at Kate, and his gaze lingered a little longer on her face than was strictly professional. He wasn't inappropriate but obviously a healthy, heterosexual man appreciating a beautiful woman. It dawned on Liam that Kate Macintyre probably had that effect on most men who crossed her path. His colleagues were cases in point.

Liam cleared his throat.

"Would you like some wine?" Liam opened the cordovan-colored leather-bound list of offerings that the server handed him and glanced at it. "I can't indulge because I have to get back to the hospital after lunch, but please go ahead."

"I love wine," she said. "But if I have a glass right now, I'll have to go home and take a nap. I'm such a lightweight. So no, thank you. I'll just have iced tea."

Liam snapped the list shut and their gazes connected. It was her eyes that exuded the warmth, he realized. Even though they turned down slightly at the outer edges, they were kind eyes that always seemed to be smiling.

The way they sparkled made him think that she would probably be a fun person—an optimist…or even an instigator, but in a good way.

Not to mention her eyes were the most beautiful shade of blue. An azure iris rimmed by a navy border. A color combination that made you look longer, trying to figure out just what made them so striking.

And it was then he realized that, like their waiter, he also had been staring a hair too long.

"Two iced teas, then," he said and handed over the wine list before the server left to get their drinks.

"So, as I was saying a minute ago," he continued. "I'm sorry for being so difficult. Sometimes it's a challenge getting the kids ready and out the door in time for school. Do you have any children?"

She held the menu open in front of her, but her gaze held his. For a split second he thought the light in her eyes dimmed a bit. "No, no children of my own. But my brother and his wife have a son. I love my nephew, Cody, as fiercely as if he were my own. He's the reason my family decided to get involved with expanding the services the hospital offers to children, but that's another story.

"What's important is that I understand why you might feel uncomfortable about the bachelor auction. I didn't realize any of the staff had children." She tilted her head to the side and quirked a brow. "Not that anything about this auction will be scandalous. It will be completely G-rated, I assure you."

"No scandal, huh?" he asked.

She shook her head. "None. Maybe a little mischief…"

As the words hung between them, she bit her lower lip, and her blue eyes danced with what Liam imagined might be all the mischief she claimed the auction lacked. For a fraction of a second, he contemplated what sort of mischief might be running through her mind.

Until she said, "I do have my own reputation to consider. Maybe we should go light on the mischief, too. Especially because I don't want to scare you off. Please know I was only joking."

She reached out and touched his hand. Her skin was soft and warm.

"Of course," he said, backpedaling from all thoughts of mischief and her soft, warm skin as fast as he could, especially when she pulled her hand away.

"Why don't we figure out what we want to eat," he said. "Then I'm eager to hear about this new plan."

Kate studied the menu so that she could regroup and gather her thoughts.

She was nervous, hence the babbling on about nonsense. Why was she suddenly so uneasy? Liam Thayer was reserved and maybe a bit gruff, but that was nothing to get anxious over, she reminded herself as she perused the menu.

Normally she was a pro at meetings like this. Just what was it about Dr. Liam Thayer that threw her off her game? Maybe she was a little worried about suggesting her alternative plan. It was a paradox, really. She stood behind this bachelor auction event.

As she'd said to Liam, it wasn't anything scandalous. She wasn't asking Celebration Memorial's doctors to perform like Chippendales. When she'd discovered that the seven of them were single, she'd simply grabbed on to the obvious fund-raising opportunity. Because what single woman in Dallas wouldn't want a date with a handsome doctor?

However, what she'd failed to factor in was that *single* didn't necessarily mean each and every one of them would be available...or elated by the idea. The possibility of any of them having kids or girlfriends hadn't even entered her mind. It was a dumb oversight, and she was lucky that only Liam had balked.

She knew how protective her brother, Rob, had been of Cody before he'd met and married Pepper. Kids changed everything. Because Kate hadn't taken that into consideration, she was determined to make this right with Liam. She was going to make sure he had the opportunity to be on good terms with his boss and to look out for the best interests of his daughters.

They made small talk about different menu items. They'd both eaten at the restaurant before—no surprise because it was enjoyed by most of the people in Celebration—and pointed out their favorite dishes to each other. Finally, after she ordered the plank-grilled salmon with seasonal vegetables and he ordered the wild mushroom ravioli with a wedge salad, she said, "So tell me. What exactly is it about the bachelor auction that you object to?"

He didn't answer her right away, and his expression was so neutral that she couldn't get a read on what he might be thinking.

"I hope that doesn't sound insensitive, but I have to ask, because I have a feeling what it might be," she said, filling the silence. "Yet I don't want to assume."

She forced herself to stop talking. It was an uncomfortable question made worse by his continued silence, but she needed to know. Especially if they were going to get past the awkwardness and move on to something that worked. She held her breath, forcing herself to be quiet until he answered.

Finally he did. "It was exactly what I told you yesterday. I have kids. I think it sets a bad example."

"Do you have boys or girls?"

He frowned. "Does it really matter?"

"No, but I'm interested."

A raised brow and a vague light that passed over his face had her stomach doing an odd clenching number, and she was suddenly scrambling to clarify.

What? Did he think she was interested in him?

"What I mean is…I'm *curious*."

He was drumming his fingers on the table. He looked down at his hands for a moment, then back up at her. She worried that the wall he'd erected around himself yesterday in the meeting might go back up. But then he blew out a breath and said, "I have two girls, Amanda and Calee. They're thirteen-year-old twins."

"Aah, twin girls," she said. "That's so sweet. I wouldn't mind having twins someday. But they don't run in our family, plus it's unlikely I'll even get married anytime soon."

What was wrong with her today? Had she left her filter at home?

Liam didn't say anything. But his gaze bore into hers, and the heat from it warmed her cheeks. Obviously Liam Thayer wasn't interested in her genetic predisposition or her hopes and aspirations for the future beyond raising funds for the children's surgical wing. His actions up to now suggested he might not even be interested in hearing about that.

Still, he had agreed to meet her for lunch.

He had a restless, intense edge about him—drumming his fingers once again on the table, scowling, shifting in his seat, glancing at his phone. She wondered if the man knew how to loosen up. Yet she hadn't really been around him for any length of time to get a realistic read on him. He was working today. As a doctor, that meant he was on the clock even on his lunch hour. He was probably anxious to get back.

When he wasn't looking through her with that piercing gaze, he seemed vaguely annoyed with her, as if it should be clear that she was taking up his precious time.

She knew she shouldn't take it personally. He'd been through a lot of trauma losing his wife. Now he was raising two teenage girls on his own. She wondered if he was this stern with them at home. Teenagers needed room to grow, to try on different attitudes and personas. But she wasn't here to offer parenting advice. Besides, that definitely wasn't her field of expertise. She was just here to do her job, and that required focus.

Regrouping her thoughts, she decided to stick to her spiel about the pediatric wing. Although, to get to the heart of why she'd asked him to meet her today, she would need to delve into his personal life a little. She braced herself and decided to dive in.

"Do you think the auction will send a bad message to your girls, or is it the date afterward that bothers you?"

She had such mixed emotions. What a lonely life it would be for someone like Liam to take himself off the market. However, she suspected it was the date more so than the auction that bothered him. And the alternative plan she was ready to propose to him hinged on him not wanting to go through with the post-auction date.

"As I've said before, the event will be tastefully done, and your children won't be there to see their father being auctioned off. It's being taped for an episode of *Catering to Dallas,* but that show won't air for several weeks."

His gaze darkened a bit. She felt like her persistence might be pushing him away. She hadn't meant to be pushy or to make him feel as if she were doing a high-pressure sales pitch on him. Again she forced herself to stay quiet through another awkward silence.

"Actually, my daughters don't watch much television. But truth be told, they're sort of excited about the auction. They know the daughter of one of my colleagues. Since her father is doing it, they want me to join in. Still, I suppose it's the post-auction date that bothers me. My wife hasn't even been gone two years. The girls have taken the loss of their mother hard. I don't want to add to their grief by going out with someone new. I don't think they fully comprehend this auction means I will take someone out on a date."

"That's perfectly understandable. I'm so sorry for your loss, Liam. I can't even imagine how difficult that must be."

He lowered his gaze again, toying with the edge of his napkin, finally taking it off the table and putting it in his lap.

There were different kinds of loss and different kinds of pain that went hand in hand with them. Kate had known the pain of losing both her parents and watching her nephew, Cody, recover from the accident that had claimed his grandfather's life. Before her father's death, she'd watched him sink into a dark, drunken depression over the loss of her mother.

She'd also known the pain of losing an unborn child. But the miscarriage wasn't something she allowed herself to think about at great lengths—because that inevitably led her to the memory of the engagement she'd walked away from, and...well, it really was like Pandora's box, and she didn't want to open it.

Still she couldn't fathom what it must be like to lose a spouse...a soul mate. The mother of the children over whom Liam was so protective. She felt bad for him, but since she was already batting a thousand today, she decided to spit out the proposition before she lost her nerve.

"Were you serious when you said you would be willing to write a check to the foundation in lieu of participating?"

His demeanor brightened. "Yes, that's what I'd prefer to do."

"Here's what I'm thinking," she said. "As you know,

Dr. Dunlevy is adamant that every senior staff member participate in the auction—especially you, since you're in charge of pediatrics. How would you feel if I bid on you with the funds from that check you are so eager to write? For all intents and purposes, you will be auctioned off. You'll look great in the eyes of your boss, but you won't have to go through with the post-auction date. Essentially you will buy your freedom. But that part will be our little secret. What do you say, Dr. Thayer?"

Chapter Four

It was a brilliant idea.

It was pure genius, and for a moment, it was as if a huge weight had been lifted off his shoulders.

"I think it's a fabulous plan," he said. "You're really willing to do that for me?"

She beamed her one-thousand-watt smile. "I wouldn't have offered if I didn't mean it."

However, as they ate their lunch, the initial relief wore off, and Liam found himself doing internal battle with a barrage of logistical questions. One of the most pervasive was whether he should offer to take her to dinner or provide some sort of post-auction compensation...as a thank-you. After all, he was enjoying their lunch and her company. A casual dinner wouldn't be so bad since she knew exactly where he was coming from—that he wasn't interested in anything more than friendship.

Thinking about the possibility that gorgeous Kate Macintyre might be interested in him as more than just a friend made him feel foolish and presumptuous. That was enough proof that the dating game was way out of his league. He'd be better off simply donating a little extra to the cause.

"I realize my colleagues will be paying for a date," he said. "I understand that the money they spend on the night out will not go directly to the hospital—the guys will spend it on the women who win them in the auction. Since I won't be paying for a date, I'm happy to donate the money I would have spent. It will go to the cause rather than be wasted on an evening on the town."

That hadn't come out quite right. His trepidation about dating sounded so ridiculous when he voiced it, but that embarrassment was at odds with the betrayal of Joy that pierced his heart when he thought of going through the motions of a date. Even if said date was contrived and a woman was bidding on a prize package—not really the time spent with him so much— the winning bidder still deserved to have a good time. Enthusiasm and interest were not something he could promise to deliver.

"What I'm trying to say is that I'm happy to donate more if you think that's appropriate. Especially since I'm obviously being a colossal pain in the... Well, I've created more work for you, and I'm sorry about that."

She laughed. "You're not a colossal pain in the... Just get over that, okay?"

She caught her bottom lip between her teeth. She did that a lot. There was something kind of innocently sexy about it. She had nice lips; the kind that he imagined could be described as bee-stung.

"As I said," she continued. "I wouldn't have offered

this alternative if I didn't think it was a win-win situation for all involved. We're good, right?"

She was so gracious. She obviously had a natural talent that put people at ease. Not to mention a pretty face to go along with the nice personality.

His gaze dropped back to the bottom lip that had just a moment ago been caught between her teeth.

"So, this new plan—you bidding on me—isn't going to cause problems with a boyfriend? I don't want to put you in an uncomfortable position...."

"Don't worry," she said. "I'm absolutely single. No jealous guys will be hulking around threatening to beat you up. Rest assured."

She winked at him, and there was something in the gesture that made the blood course through his veins in a way that hadn't happened in ages.

"Really? Have you ever been married?" He surprised himself by uttering the words out loud. "And that's really personal. You don't have to answer that question if you'd rather not."

She had a serene smile on her face, as if his inquiry hadn't fazed her.

"I don't mind answering," she said. "As long as you'll answer a question for me."

Liam was vaguely aware of the muted background chatter of other customers, silverware clattering on plates, coffee cups clanking on saucers. Background music to their conversation.

"Fair enough," he said.

"I've never been married. I came close once, but... nope. Lately I've been too busy with work to date much. I figure I'm sort of married to my career right now. Kind of like a doctor, huh?"

"Is that the question you wanted me to answer? Because, if so, it's a lot easier than I expected."

She laughed. "Are you kidding? That's a rhetorical question, and you know it. What I want to know is why, if your daughters are okay with you doing the auction, do you still want to go through with the charade of me bidding on you? Which I'm perfectly willing to do. But, again, I'm curious.

"Because it's just a night out. You really don't even have to call it a *date*. It's not like you're obligated to see her again. How painful could one night out with a woman be?"

Liam shook his head. "I don't know how to say this without sounding like a pompous ass, but I'll do my best. There might be women or, should I say, one woman in particular, who would be tempted to bid on me just to put me in an uncomfortable situation."

Kate didn't say anything, but the corner of her mouth quirked up as if she thought the possibility utterly ridiculous. "Would you care to elaborate?"

"Shortly after Joy died—Joy was my wife…" His voice cracked, and he wondered if he would really be better off not venturing into this territory.

Kate's expression softened. "I think everyone in Celebration knew and loved your wife, Liam. She was an amazing woman."

He cleared his throat. "She *was* an amazing woman. I think that's part of the problem. Some women think a man like me, who is left to raise two teenage girls alone, needs or wants help."

"And you're speaking from experience?"

Liam felt himself sliding down a slippery slope. "Nah, never mind." He didn't need to unload his baggage on Kate. He should be telling her how grateful he was for her willingness to make his part in this fundraiser as easy and comfortable as possible. But he'd already said too much. It was best to quit while he was ahead.

"No, wait, this sounds good. So you're in demand? Throngs of females throwing themselves at you?" Her eyes were sparkling, and her tone was teasing.

He was sure she was just trying to lighten the mood, but it wasn't something he wanted to joke about.

"And you need me to fight off the hordes of women that will turn out to bid on you?"

He crossed his arms. "I wouldn't put it that way."

She pressed a finger to her chin and narrowed her eyes as if she were thinking. "Maybe I shouldn't bid on you. Maybe I should be quiet and watch as the bidding war ensues."

"There won't be a bidding war," Liam said. "And you already offered to bid on me. No reneging on the deal."

"You realize that me bidding on you won't preempt a bidding war. That's all on you, and if it happens, there isn't a thing I can do to stop it. We'll all just sit back and watch Dr. Thayer bring sexy back."

He laughed, unsure whether the burning sensation he felt was the blood rushing to or draining from his face. He reached up and ran his hand over his chin as if he could rub away the evidence of his embarrassment.

"Maybe this is a bad idea," he said.

She reached out and touched his arm again. "I'm just teasing, Liam. I know you've been through a lot, but I was hoping this might be a chance for you to have some fun. We have a deal, and I fully intend to uphold my end of the bargain."

She opened her mouth as if she were going to say something, but closed it and sat back in her chair.

"What?" he asked, wondering why he was encouraging her.

She put both of her palms flat on the table. "Okay, I'm just going to say it. You're a young man. You have a lot of life ahead of you. I didn't know Joy very well. We only met once in passing, but the little I did know of her was that she was a sweet, kind woman. I can't imagine that she would want you to put yourself on a shelf for the rest of your life."

The truth hung between them as acrid as the smell of something burning. Kate was right, as much as he hated to admit it. Joy probably would've wanted him to move on, to meet someone wonderful, who would love the girls like Joy did and for him to fall in love again.

There were two things wrong with that. First, he and Joy had never had the chance to discuss whether or not she wanted him to remarry should anything happen to her—or vice versa for that matter. He hadn't expected his thirty-five-year-old wife to run out to the store for vanilla ice cream and never come back. Second, nobody would ever love their girls the way Joy did. And unfortunately he'd had firsthand experience with that, compliments of Kimela Herring.

He cleared his throat. "I'm working on that. Sort of. I'm going to grief counseling, but I can't say it's helping. In fact I don't know how long I'll continue. But after Joy died, I had a bad experience. One of her friends started coming around. At first she seemed to have good intentions, but then she started moving a little too fast, pushing a little too hard. She did a lot of damage because she didn't always tell the truth, and she lied because she didn't have the girls' best interests at heart.

"I really don't want to talk about the details, but it didn't end well. It probably wasn't her fault. I was still too numb from losing Joy to know what I was doing, much less what Kimela was up to. But that's no excuse. I had no business getting involved with anyone. For that reason I've decided I won't date until the girls go off to college. That's just five years."

"Is this the woman you're afraid might bid on you?"

Liam nodded, then shrugged. "She probably won't. It sounds egotistical for me to even say such a thing. I made her pretty mad, and she hasn't spoken to me since. Really I don't even know why I brought it up."

Kate stared at her hands, which, Liam noticed, were long and slender and nicely manicured. "I'm sorry you and the girls had to go through that on top of the pain and grief you suffered after losing Joy. That must've been difficult."

"It was. Still is." Liam shrugged again. "I hope I don't sound conceited acting like all the women in Dallas will be lined up to bid on me. It's just that I don't want to give anyone the wrong idea like I did with Kimela. And I do want you to know how much I appreciate your kindness."

"I'm sorry if I sounded like I was making light of the situation earlier." They looked at each other and something passed between them.

She smiled her kind smile, then arched her brow in that way that was beginning to make *him* smile.

"Please know I would never throw you to the wolf— or the wolves."

They both laughed at this. It was nice how it lightened the mood.

"Well, then I'll owe you big-time," he said.

She shook her head. "You being in the auction is payment enough. But if you really feel beholden, what you can do is help me come up with the date package that we can say you're offering."

"Ah, the old fake prize package," he said. He studied her for a moment as he tried to figure out what kind of date would appeal to a woman like Kate Macintyre. An elegant woman of class and style who seemed to have it all together... What would she like? Where would she like to go?

"Since you'll be the recipient of this pretend date, where would you like to go? A weekend at a vineyard? An excursion on a private yacht?"

"Hold on there, sailor, you're talking a little extravagant. You might want to rein it in a bit. Women are already lining up to bid on you."

"No, we don't want that," he said.

He grinned and shook his head. He liked her quick wit and sharp sense of humor. She had an ease about her that helped him to not take himself so seriously and relax more than he'd been able to in a long time.

"What kind of bachelor auction dream-date package would you bid on?"

"My dream date would be a little more low-key. I'm not a froufrou kind of gal."

"Really? No froufrou? You look like the kind of woman who would enjoy a nice night on the town."

"At the risk of sounding completely boring, give me no-nonsense back-to-nature time, where I can enjoy some peace and quiet and the person I'm with. That's my idea of a good day. Maybe throw in some wine or champagne. I could go for that."

"Sounds perfect."

"The only other thing besides the date write-up that I'll need from you is a short bio with a photo for the program and publicity. I can send over a photographer to get the shot if you don't have one."

The last formal pic he'd had taken was a family portrait that Joy had arranged where the two of them and the girls were wearing jeans and white shirts. They were all barefoot, which he didn't understand, but it was what Joy had wanted. They were in the Main Street Park and the bougainvillea had been flourishing that day, brimming over with hot pink blossoms. Joy had been so excited about the explosion of color that she had insisted they had to go right then, before the blooms were off the bushes. The thought made him smile to himself.

That was the thing about Joy; she'd always seized the moment. She didn't put things off for another day.

Sadness eclipsed the smile in his heart. Had she somehow known on some mysterious, subconscious level that she had to get things done as fast as she could…because she wouldn't have much time in this world?

"Are you okay?" Kate asked. "Seems like I lost you there for a minute. The picture? Do you have one we can use?"

He shrugged. "I'll look, but the only pictures of myself that come to mind are the ones that scream *family man*. That definitely seems at odds with this cause."

"I don't know. Being a family man is a good quality. You don't have to hide it."

"The main photo I'm thinking of is a family portrait. Joy and the girls are in it with me. I guess I should clarify up front that I want to leave my daughters out of this and Joy, too, for that matter. I don't want any mention of them in the bio or other auction material. Deal?"

"Absolutely. In fact, we'll make your bio as bare-bones as possible to discourage the voting."

He wished he could be as confident as she was.

She smiled. "Don't worry, okay? This is going to turn out fine."

It was strange, but the earnest look in her eyes gave him the spark of hope he had thought he would never feel again.

Chapter Five

When Liam walked up to check in at the nurses' station to let the crew know he was back from lunch, Cullen Dunlevy was standing there reading over something. Liam had managed to avoid the man all morning. Good thing, too. If Cullen had jumped on him about the auction this morning before Liam had had a chance to meet with Kate, Liam would have been singing a completely different tune. Now he was armed and ready.

"Cullen," Liam greeted his boss, as he walked past him to move the magnet on the master On Duty board hanging on the wall.

"Liam." Cullen's voice had an edge, and he wore a determined look that suggested he was in the mood to argue. "Have you given any more thought to what we talked about yesterday?"

Liam grimaced at a *Win a Date with a Doctor* flyer advertising the pediatric wing benefit; it was taped to the bottom of the in/out board. He was really going through with this stunt. Well, sort of. Thanks to Kate and her brilliance. The woman was not only beautiful, she was intelligent. And funny and compassionate.

She was racing against the clock to pull together all the pieces of this auction so it could take place in just a little over a week. Yet she had time to accommodate his special needs. He might've felt guilty if he hadn't been so grateful to her.

As he slid the small black circle from the *out* square to the one that indicated he was *in* and back to work, Liam couldn't resist the urge to yank Cullen's chain a little. He wouldn't give in to the guy that easily. "And which conversation would that be, Cullen?" He picked up a clipboard off the desk and started making notes, taking care to keep his eyes down and his voice dispassionate.

"The fund-raiser," Cullen replied flatly.

"Fund-raiser?"

"*Yes,* the *fund-raiser.* You know what I'm talking about, Dr. Thayer." The subtext was *Don't be an ass.* "The bachelor auction that's happening a week from tomorrow at the Regency Cypress Plantation."

"Oh, that fund-raiser." Liam turned and started walking away. "Yeah. I'm in," he said over his shoulder.

"You are?" Cullen asked.

When Liam turned back around to revel in the look on his boss's face, he saw that the two nurses behind the desk were gaping at them as if they were watching two players volley in the last game of a tennis match.

"Sure," Liam returned. "Unless you've decided you don't need me."

"And were you going to inform me of this decision, or were you just going to surprise me and show up?"

"Sometimes surprises are a good thing, Dr. Dunlevy. Don't knock them. They keep life interesting."

Kate's "clandestine bid" plan had surprised him. Thanks to her, he could "represent" his department—as Cullen had put it—without the pressures that came from the aftermath of the auction. What had once seemed like a very sharp thorn in his side was turning out to be an interesting exercise in "Where there's a will, there's a way." And he loved the way Kate's mind worked. He appreciated the way she hadn't gotten frustrated with him or simply written him off. Hell, he'd been such a pain in the ass that he would've written himself off.

He owed Kate much more than the five-thousand-dollar check he'd promised to write and deliver within the next couple days; apparently that was the going rate for auctioned bachelors.

Now he owed her a huge debt of gratitude for this stroke of genius. Or at least another lunch at Luigi's… or perhaps dinner. But they'd cross that bridge when they came to it.

Right now he had patients to see, and Kate had left him with two assignments: he had to find a picture of himself for the website and program, and he had to come up with a description of the faux date he was offering. Something similar to the write-ups his colleagues had already penned and posted, detailing what they were offering.

What if the prize package he offered was a simple dinner for two? He appreciated Kate's advice.

Don't make the night out sound too exciting. The object is not to make yourself too tempting and irresistible. If you think you can manage that.

He liked her sense of humor, how she didn't take herself too seriously. Even thinking about this made him smile as he started his afternoon rounds.

Kate's phone rang at 9:00 a.m. on Saturday morning. When she saw Liam's name pop up on her cell phone's caller ID, her heart lurched, and for a split second, her breath caught under her ribs.

But she recovered fast enough, blaming the visceral reaction on the fear that he'd changed his mind after he'd had time to mull over the plan that they had agreed on yesterday.

Then, as her finger hovered over the button to answer the call, she felt a little ridiculous because she had no reason to believe he'd back out. He'd given his word. He was on board. It was just that she'd become so attached to the idea of having all seven of the hospital's single doctors participate in the auction. Even though the show would go on without him. It just wouldn't be the same....

"Hello?" she said, taking care to steady her voice.

"Good morning, Kate," he said. "It's Liam. I hope I'm not calling too early."

"I'm already in the office."

"On Saturday? Do you ever take a break?"

He had the type of masculine voice she loved: deep, rich and smooth...like velvet. She had to admit to herself that she was a little mesmerized by it.

"The auction is right around the corner, and there's a lot to get done," she said. "So no breaks for me until the last bid is cast."

"Actually that's why I'm calling," he said.

She held her breath.

"I need to talk to you about the auction," he said.

"Would it be all right if I dropped by your office this morning?"

"That depends," she said. "It's fine as long as you promise you're not coming by to tell me you've changed your mind. If that's the case, then I'm completely swamped today. In fact I won't be available until I see you at the Regency Cypress Plantation on the day of the auction."

She was only half joking.

And she was so relieved when he laughed.

"No, I'm not calling to back out. I promise. So can I come by? I want to bring you the check. I'll even bring coffee."

After Liam dropped off Amanda and Calee at the dance studio, he put the top down on his 1965 Mustang ragtop, programmed the address on Kate's business card into his GPS and pointed his car in the direction of downtown Dallas.

It had been ages since he'd driven with the top down. Certainly not since Joy had been gone. But today the sky was robin's-egg-blue. There wasn't a cloud in sight, and the air was the perfect temperature. How could he resist? If a person owned a convertible and *didn't* put down the top on a day like this, they should be arrested or, at the very least, be forced to surrender the vehicle to someone who knew how to use it.

When he pulled out onto the highway, he had the wind in his face and the roar of the white noise in his ears. For the first time in what seemed forever he couldn't even hear the thoughts in his head that usually wouldn't let him be.

For a few minutes it was as if he'd stepped outside himself. God, it was freeing. But then, as he neared Dallas, as the green gave way to the concrete of the city, the world began to close in again. Still, that was all right; it had been a good escape. It sort of felt like a breakthrough, as if he'd been paroled from the prison of his mind. Even if it was just for a few glorious moments.

Now, as he searched for a coffee place, he thought about the pictures in the manila envelope which he'd stuck in the glove compartment. He'd spent the better part of last night digging up possible photos of himself for Kate to use for the auction publicity. Perusing the family albums had been a daunting task but surprisingly not as difficult as he'd imagined. Before he'd forced himself to sit down and do it, he'd thought that looking at pictures of Joy, so happy and full of life—with the girls, with him, unaware that her life would be cut so cruelly short…in the blink of an eye—would've been a heartbreaking task. Instead, what he walked away with was a feeling of how short life is, how fleeting. There's not enough time to waste a second of what lies ahead.

That's why, when the flawless morning had greeted him, he had decided to put the top down and enjoy it. He'd wanted to right when the girls had climbed in the car, but they had fussed that they'd spent too much time slicking their hair back into the requisite ballerina buns that were required for class. All that would be undone by the time they drove there.

He was feeling too light to argue. So the minute they disappeared behind the front doors of the dance studio, he'd put the top down and sped off to enjoy the beautiful morning. And his meeting with Kate.

He could've emailed the photos to her. He could've mailed her the check. But he didn't.

He contemplated the excuse that if he'd scanned and emailed the pictures last night, she would get them instantaneously and would put them up on the website right away. The longer he held on to the photos, the less time his mug would be up for humiliation on the auction homepage.

Plus he wanted Kate's opinion on which picture to use. She was the only person he'd trust with this. Kate understood his trepidations. She seemed to get what he was up against as a single dad raising two teenage daughters.

He found a coffee shop with a drive-through, placed his order, then drove to Kate's office. He parked in a garage, then set out walking toward her office with the drink tray balanced in his hands and a large manila envelope tucked underneath his arm containing a check for five thousand dollars, a flash drive of scanned digital photos and printed copies of the pictures.

Kate's office was housed in a modern glass-and-chrome skyscraper. As he tugged open the building's door, it hit him that, despite the building's cold modernity, Kate seemed to place the same value on family that he did. When she'd spoken of hers, she'd mentioned her brother and his family, but she'd also said it was unlikely she'd get married anytime soon.

Why hadn't someone snatched her up? She seemed like a good catch.

He wished everyone could experience what he'd had with Joy. But some people weren't that lucky.

Love was a mysterious and magical thing, and he was darned lucky to have found it with Joy, no matter how short their time together had been.

He'd had his great love. Since some people never found that kind of love at all, he had to be happy with having experienced it once in his lifetime.

As the door closed behind him and he stepped inside

the massive glass lobby, the golden glow of the mid-morning sun gave way to the odd greenish cast caused by light filtering through the building's glass structure. The shift in atmosphere was nearly palpable; an odd, oppressive reminder that the true-love chapter of his life was closed. The realization weighed on him like something heavy and cruel.

Maybe a delayed hangover from last night's trip down memory lane was finally settling over him. Maybe he was being truthful with himself about why he'd driven all this way.

He was here to see Kate—even if he'd told himself that he'd only come seeking her help with choosing a picture. Since that was the case, there was no reason to feel uncomfortable.

He glanced around the lobby and looked up. The ceiling seemed to stretch on for miles above his head. The glass and plants created a green-tinged light, the same hue that was found in old-fashioned soda bottles. It poured in from all directions and reflected off the chrome furniture, chrome fixtures and giant chrome fountain that dominated the majority of the building's first floor. Everything about the space was sleek and cold and slightly damp.

As he looked around for a directory to help him locate the foundation offices, he was struck by how opposite the place was to Kate's personality. She was warm and personable. She drew people to her, whereas this place was hard, cold and impersonal. It was as if he'd fallen to the bottom of some great glass aquarium and had no way out.

"May I help you, sir?"

Liam looked to his right and spied a receptionist stationed behind a glass-and-chrome desk right in front of a bank of elevators.

He hesitated a moment, unsure of why he suddenly felt the need to escape. He could just say, "No thanks," and walk out. But why? After he'd come all this way. And Kate was expecting him.

"Yes," he answered as he turned and walked toward the security desk. "I'm looking for the Macintyre Family Foundation offices."

"Do you have an appointment?" The tall, slim, attractive brunette flashed a perfect pearly-white smile. Whoever was in charge of staffing cared about making a good first impression.

"Yes. Kate Macintyre is expecting me."

From the way the receptionist regarded him with that polite-but-guarded smile, it was clear that no one got past the gatekeeper without having a reason to be here.

"One moment, please." The brunette picked up the phone, a sleek cordless model. Before she dialed she asked, "Your name, please?"

"Liam Thayer."

As the woman spoke to the person on the other end of the line, Liam looked around. The place was impressive, a monument to the empire Rob Macintyre had built. Liam was glad he'd done the research and knew of the Macintyre family's humble beginnings. If he didn't know better, he might believe that he and Kate had come from polar-opposite worlds.

"You may go right up," said the brunette. "The foundation's executive offices are on the twenty-fifth floor."

She handed Liam a visitor's pass and directed him to an elevator that carried him up without stopping. The doors opened into a space where the vaguely green-tinged glow radiated through more floor-to-ceiling windows.

"Hi, Liam." Kate was standing in front of him looking gorgeous in a casual red blouse and blue jeans that hugged her curves like a second skin. "It's so nice to see you."

From what he could tell, they were the only two in the office. "It's nice to see you, too."

Liam stood there grasping the edges of the drink tray, his mouth suddenly dry. Why the hell had he come here? He felt like he was being unfaithful. But Joy was gone and the girls... This had nothing to do with *the girls*.

He cleared his throat. "I brought you something." The words came out in one swift, brusque statement. Still balancing the drink tray on one hand, he held out the envelope to her.

He realized he probably should've offered her the coffee first.

"What's this?" she asked.

As she took the envelope from him, their hands brushed, and she looked up at him and smiled, raising her right eyebrow in a way that was both tantalizing and disconcerting as hell. That combination of feelings pushed him way out of his comfort zone—the barrier that being married and having a family had always provided. Now he existed in some strange no-man's-land: no longer married, but not free of heart, either. Sometimes he felt as if he had no idea what the hell he was doing anymore.

"They're pictures," he said. "For the bachelor auction. I thought you could pick the one you liked best. But first, have some coffee. Fortify yourself. You'll probably need it."

She shook her head and laughed as she accepted the

cup he offered her. A dimple he hadn't noticed before winked at him from her right cheek.

"Come into my office," she said, motioning him to follow.

He did, like a child behind the Pied Piper. Only it was very much on his mind that, by coming here today, he was a consenting adult. He made a conscious effort to keep his gaze on the back of Kate's head, not allowing it to meander any lower than her shoulders, especially not to the curves outlined by those tight jeans.

She led him to a large office down a long hallway. When they stepped inside, even though the room had floor-to-ceiling windows similar to the ones in the building's lobby and the foundation's reception area, Kate's office had a warmer feeling, fostered by traditional furniture: a desk, credenza and a couch with two upholstered chairs arranged around a coffee table made out of the same rich-toned wood as the desk. Several paintings created in the Impressionist style hung on the walls, a sharp contrast to the spectacular view of the Dallas skyline outside her windows.

"This is where I live these days." She gestured wide with both arms. "Welcome to my humble office."

"Nice place."

"Thank you." She took a seat on the far end of the couch, leaving him the choice to join her or park himself in one of the chairs. He figured since they would be looking at photos, it made more sense to sit next to her.

He settled himself on the couch, propping his left ankle on his right knee, leaving the middle cushion free between them.

She sipped her coffee.

"Here," he said, gesturing to the drink holder he'd placed on the coffee table right next to where she'd placed the envelope of pictures. "There's cream and sugar, if you'd like some. I forgot to ask how you took your coffee. So I asked for a little bit of everything."

It struck him how personal and intimate it was, knowing what a person put in their coffee. Not privately personal, but it was an individual's taste, one of the many parts that added up to the whole. One small piece of the puzzle of daily life that made the person tick, and a tidbit that so many people took for granted.

"I'd love a little cream, thank you." Kate leaned in and set her cup on a stone coaster—which featured line drawings of Paris-scapes—and removed the lid. She poured half-and-half into the hot liquid. Liam watched it lighten as she stirred.

Kate took her coffee with cream. As she curled her legs under her on her end of the couch, Liam filed the fact away for future reference.

"Thank you for bringing this." She raised her cup to him.

"You bet."

He touched the edge of his cup to hers. The cold feeling of trepidation he'd had when he had entered the building's lobby melted away in the warmth of her smile.

"I have to confess," she said. "When I asked you to lunch yesterday to tell you about my plan, I was so nervous. I thought for sure you were going to shoot it down."

"Well, you looked very brave, then. I had no idea you were nervous."

He made her nervous? That was surprising and a little bit endearing.

"Anyone would be nervous if they thought their grand plan would be rejected."

"I wouldn't reject you, Kate."

He'd said the words before he realized how they sounded, before he realized that he meant them.

"Are you sure about that?" she asked.

And a light of understanding seemed to pass between them.

It was crazy. It made no sense at all. He'd known this woman for three days, and here he was…here they were. One moment he was compelled to drive to Dallas to see her; the next moment he was reminding himself not to be greedy—that he'd had the love of his life in Joy. That chapter—the chapter of falling in love and being head-over-heels crazy for someone—was finished.

Yet every time he saw Kate, his life felt like he'd been handed a fresh, clean blank page ready for a new story.

"You obviously need to give yourself more credit," he said. "It was a great plan."

She bit her bottom lip and glanced up at him, her blue, blue eyes searching through dark thick lashes.

"Thank you," she said.

"It was a surprise when I talked to my daughters and found out they weren't at all bothered by the idea of their old man being auctioned off. I guess sometimes I form conclusions too fast. Or maybe I'm just a little too overprotective."

"Don't apologize for being a good parent," Kate said. "I told you how I love my nephew like he was my own. My brother is the same way, fiercely protective. It's definitely better to be overly cautious than to wish you would've been."

For nearly two years Liam had been overly cautious, protecting his girls, guarding his heart. He'd vowed not to get involved with anyone until the girls were off at school…if even then. Since he'd walked into that staff meeting, it felt as if life were making a point: Liam didn't get to schedule when he would meet a person he was interested in.

Was that what was happening to him now?

He was glad when she picked up the envelope off the coffee table and removed its contents.

"Thank you for this," she said, holding up the check.

"It's the least I can do," he said.

She shuffled through the photos, pausing when she got to the black-and-white 5x7 professional headshot that the hospital kept on hand for publicity purposes.

She held it up and pulled a disapproving look. "Really, Liam? You need to get a better picture taken."

He shrugged. "I thought it might suffice in a pinch. It's the one the hospital uses for publicity. Technically this event is hospital publicity. So that shot should work perfectly."

"Only if you want to drive people away."

"It's not *that* bad."

She leaned in and held it next to his face. As she did, he could smell her shampoo, something clean and fresh and slightly floral. Mixed with her perfume, she smelled quite tantalizing. He inhaled deeply, and awareness flooded through him with an almost painful intensity.

He reached up and took the photo from her, and, as he had hoped, she settled back onto her side of the couch. He was relieved to have reclaimed his personal space.

"So this one's out, huh? And none of the other shots work?"

She picked up the stack of snapshots. "I don't know. Let me look again."

"You certainly didn't seem very bowled over by them the first time through. You know, not everyone is photogenic. Have mercy on me."

She shot him a sidelong glance. "You could be very photogenic." She held up the picture of him and Joy on a trip to the Bahamas about three years ago. "You look great here."

They both studied the picture silently. It was as if neither of them wanted to be the first to suggest that Joy should be cropped out. He was suddenly sorry he'd brought pictures of him with her. But he didn't really have any without her. He should've done the cropping after he had scanned in the shots. The reality had hulked in the back of his mind; however, he couldn't pull the thought to the forefront and face it.

"She was really beautiful, Liam," Kate said. "You know, I met her once. I didn't put the pieces together until after I'd left the meeting. I'm sorry."

Liam didn't know what to say. *It's okay? It's not your fault?* It wasn't her fault. No matter what he said, it wouldn't change anything. He didn't want her feeling sorry for him.

They sat in silence for a moment, the picture between them. He was grateful when Kate finally frowned and shook her head. "Unfortunately this one won't work, either. You look great, but once we scan it, crop it and blow it up, it will be way too grainy. The quality would be horrendous. It would look very unprofessional."

"I'm not concerned about making myself look too good. The objective is for women *not* to vote on me. Remember? Just use this one."

He slapped the hospital head shot onto the cushion between them. "There, it's settled."

"Do you really want to look like you have a stick up your butt? Is that the image you want to project? Well, then it's your choice…. Liam, I don't mean to be mean. I'm just being honest." She pointed to the photo. "The

guy in this photo and the guy sitting next to me are...
night and day. You're a great-looking guy, Liam. Really."

Something in her manner soothed him.

He took the 5x7 photo from her and studied it again.
His expression was a little stern. And his hair was a
little longer than was stylish these days. Plus, even if
it was a hospital media photo, the white lab coat made
him look stiff and boring. She was right. The photo really was unflattering. Especially compared to some of
the pictures his colleagues had already posted to the
auction's website.

"Well, I guess I could have one taken," he said. "But
I'll have to wait until Wednesday because I have a busy
week. Do we really need to put my picture and bio up
on the website at all? Especially since I'm already spoken for."

She did that arching thing with her eyebrow once
more, and it triggered that strange magnetic pull...
again.

"Technically we should include you. The website
won't be complete if we don't. But I guess if we can't
find a good shot of you, we don't have to. Or maybe we
could delay posting it. But first let me try something."
She grabbed her phone. "Believe it or not the camera on
my smartphone is as good as some 35mm SLR cameras.
Let me snap some shots of you. Then you won't have to
go to the trouble of having one taken."

He waved away her suggestion. "No, you don't have
to bother with that. I really should let you get back to
work."

But she'd already grabbed her phone.

She smiled at him, and he saw that dimple once more.
It caused a strange tightness in his chest, and his mouth
went dry again.

Chapter Six

As Kate began snapping pictures of Liam, she watched him regress into the rigid, reserved, buttoned-up doctor she'd first met in the staff meeting earlier that week.

It was sort of a relief. Or at least it helped put everything into better perspective.

Edgy Liam was more difficult to feel for than the more human side of him that she'd glimpsed and was beginning to care for.

"Just relax, Liam," she said. "Quit fidgeting. And fix your hair. Oh, here, I'll do it."

She stepped forward to smooth down a piece that was sticking up, and her fingers brushed his temple. The minute they connected, a white-hot current zinged from his skin to hers. She pulled her hand away, reclaiming her personal space. Had he felt that, too?

Rather than wander down a road she really shouldn't travel, she thought about how it was surprising that, even though he'd reverted back to stiff, proper Dr. Liam Thayer, he'd let her groom him. He always seemed so in control. By allowing her to take his picture, he was letting her take charge. It was strange and exhilarating. And there she was heading down that dangerous road again.

She took another step back, giving herself some room to breathe, and fumbled with her cell, engaging the camera.

She held it up, centering him in the viewfinder. This time he smiled, and it seemed to reach all the way through the camera to her heart. He really was a good-looking guy.

"Okay, that's great," she said. "On the count of three. One…two…"

His lips flattened into a frown. She looked up from the camera. "Why did you stop smiling? Your expression before was perfect."

He crossed his arms over his chest, obviously forcing up the corners of his mouth. "What do you mean?"

"You know what I mean," she answered. "Before I started counting, you were smiling. When I started you stopped. Just do what you were doing before."

She looked through the lens again. Now he'd narrowed his brows, and his forehead was creased.

Really?

She lowered the camera. "Liam? Is something wrong?"

"No, does it look like it is?"

"Actually, yes. You look like you're mad or possibly in pain. You were doing great earlier. Just…smile. It's not that hard. And uncross your arms. Loosen up a little bit."

"Loosen up?"

"Yes."

He dropped his arms and shrugged.

She snapped a few shots in rapid succession, as fast as the camera would shoot.

"Like this?" Another forced smile that didn't reach his eyes.

Not exactly, but it was better.

At least he wasn't frowning.

"Maybe you should stand up? That might help you loosen up."

He stood and crossed his arms again.

"Give me something that won't embarrass your daughters. You don't want to embarrass them, do you?"

"That's not fair," he said. "Besides, why is a *good picture* so important? Why are we putting so much emphasis on looks? The last thing I want to do is reinforce that the outer image is all that matters."

"I'm sure they're smart enough to know that."

"Of course they're smart."

"Well, then, don't argue with me and give me something I can work with here."

"You want something you can work with? Okay."

He turned his back to the camera.

Wait. What? Was he trying to be funny?

"Oh, wise guy, huh?"

He glanced over his shoulder and shot her an incredulous look.

"What kind of a date would *that* expression promise? You look a little formidable." She was snapping pictures as fast as she could. That was the great thing about a digital camera. You could snap away until you ran out of space, then erase the bad ones and start all over again.

"Gee, thanks," he said. He pulled a sinister-looking

frown. "We could call this one The Fright Night package."

Click-click. Click-click. Click-click.

"That sounds fitting," she said. "What else ya got? Maybe give me something that *would* embarrass your girls."

He stood stock-still, and for a moment she worried that she might have crossed the line. But then to her surprise, Liam started mugging for the camera. She clicked the camera again before he could change his mind.

"How about a date with a super hero?" He pulled at his shirt.

Good lord, he was handsome. Even better when he wasn't taking himself so seriously.

"I'd bid on that," she said, hoping to encourage him. "What are my other choices?"

"How about *The Thinker?*" He curled his fist and braced his chin on it, like Rodin's famous statue.

"Too intellectual," she teased. "Liam, girls just want to have fun."

"Is that so?"

"Sad but true, I know. Nowadays it seems like women only want men for their bodies."

"I feel so objectified," he said, as he flexed both biceps and then pulled some cheesy bodybuilderesque poses.

Kate snapped away, amazed not only by the fact that he could be pretty funny when he let loose but that she'd never noticed how nice his arms were. How had she missed those guns until now?

The sparks of attraction ignited in her, but she squelched it. He was a good-looking man in great physical condition. What woman in her right mind wouldn't be attracted to Liam Thayer?

In between the playful shots, she'd managed to capture him laughing and smiling. She stopped shooting to review the shots she'd already taken.

Yes, she definitely had at least one that would work for the purpose that she needed. She also had a lot of funny shots.

She laughed. "All I can say is, you'd better be nice to me because, boy, have I got blackmail material right here in my hot little hands."

She held up the camera and shook it at him.

"What? Let me see."

He walked over and stood next to her. She began paging through the shots.

"Oh, my God, that's terrible," he said. "I didn't think you were really shooting the goofball shots. You have to erase those."

"I'm not going to erase them," she joked. "These could be very valuable."

"Oh, no you don't." He tried to take her phone, and a playful tug-of-war ensued. One minute they were laughing and tussling, and then the next thing she knew, his lips were skimming her cheek. Kate tilted back her head, looking up at him. His eyes were hungry and hooded. Kate wasn't sure who closed the final distance; really, it didn't matter. The next thing she knew his lips were on hers, and her hands were in his hair, pulling him to her.

The kiss lasted a lifetime, despite the fact that it was over before it had a chance to begin.

It was only a brief lock of lips that endured for a moment—the span of maybe five heartbeats—but in that time, the possibility of the rest of Liam's life flashed before his eyes.

Kate's lush, tempting mouth drew him in. And the way her lips parted as he lowered his head for a taste awakened a voracious hunger inside him. During that kiss, Liam wanted to consume her; he wanted to pull her to him so that their bodies melded into one under the intense heat of his desire. But all too soon he sensed her hesitation and pulled back.

Her gaze riveted to his, she bit her bottom lip, gaping at him with large blue eyes that seemed to be amazed and darkened with wanting. Or maybe he only imagined the desire because he so desperately wanted to lose himself in her.

Kate affected him in the same way that water eroded stone, seeping over and under and around until it wore away resistance so it could flow straight through the heart. Since Joy's death and the Kimela debacle, no one had broken through the well-constructed wall that he'd erected around his heart.

Until now.

"I should probably apologize for that," he murmured, "but I'm not really sorry."

"Then don't apologize."

He shrugged, and she smiled.

Backlit by the afternoon sun streaming in through her office window, her blond hair illuminated like a halo; she looked like an angel.

But he knew angels didn't have lips that tasted like wine or curves that tempted the mind to travel to places he really shouldn't be traversing.

No, Kate Macintyre was no guardian angel, but that didn't keep him from thinking that she still might be the one who could save him from himself. She might be the one who could help him make peace with the past and start looking toward the future.

It was just a kiss, Kate reminded herself when Liam left ten minutes later, and she was alone with her thoughts and the taste of him still fresh in her mouth. They'd lost themselves for a moment, but it was something they'd have to pretend had never happened.

He'd made it perfectly clear that he was not ready to get involved with anyone for the next five years, until after he'd sent his daughters off to college.

He hadn't said that in the moments following the kiss. No, they'd made polite small talk about the photo, the bio, the pretend date. They'd talked about everything other than what had just happened between them.

He was a good father. Who could blame him for wanting to focus on his kids? There was no arguing with that.

Maybe Kate's own pregnancy had awakened maternal feelings. She'd miscarried, but the maternal feelings and the understanding that kids came first, that family came first, had never gone away.

That's why she called off her wedding. She just couldn't do it. She couldn't marry Gibson Baker because she couldn't put him first. He was a good guy, but after the miscarriage, Kate had finally let herself accept the fact that something was missing.

Some might have called her a runaway bride, but she had done Gibson a favor by letting him go. He deserved someone who loved him. Kate didn't, not the way he deserved.

When she'd gotten pregnant, they'd both wanted to give their baby a traditional home. For a while Kate had made herself believe that the love she felt for their child was big enough that it would spill over and nourish their marriage.

After she'd lost the baby, she realized she didn't have anything left to give. It was as if everything she was ever capable of giving had died with her child.

She couldn't bring herself to marry a man she didn't love.

She'd grown up watching her parents' dysfunctional marriage. Her father had worshiped the ground her mother walked on, but her mother's heart had always belonged to someone else. Kate hadn't known the facts until long after her mother had died, but Kate had always sensed a sort of reserve in her mother, a holding back that had hurt her father and had driven him to the bottle.

After learning her mother's secret and judging by Kate's own relationships, she'd realized love was rarely an equitable exchange. One person always loved more. Kate knew from experience that it wasn't any better being the one on the receiving end, left wanting, feeling as if she wasn't capable of loving to the same depth as her partner.

She'd never felt that depth of love until the baby. When she'd lost it, all of that love died, too.

There were exceptions to the rule of nonequitable love. Her brother Rob had a terrible first marriage but seemed to have found true love and happiness with his wife, Pepper. The same went for Pepper's friends A.J., Sydney and Caroline. They were all newly married and deeply in love. The skeptic in Kate wanted to qualify that with a quip about how everyone was still enjoying the newlywed stage of the game.

Let's check back in with them in ten years or so and see how everything shakes down once the dust has settled. Not that she would delight in being right. But obviously she was more of a realist than a romantic.

Still what about Joy and Liam Thayer? Everyone knew that he was desperately in love with Joy. From all accounts it seemed that she had felt the same way.

Maybe they were the exception to the rule. Even so, if he had been the one to love more, what did the next woman who came into his life have to look forward to? Living in the shadow of his never-ending love for Joy?

So there, once again, was the burning question: Was it better to love fiercely and know that you were the one who loved more, or was it best to be the object of someone's fierce love and not be able to return the feelings at the same level of intensity?

She pressed her fingers to her bottom lip, still feeling the ghost of Liam's mouth on hers. It had been a great kiss. Electric. And she knew on some subconscious level that she'd been angling for it from the minute he'd called and said he was coming by her office.

She was the one who had urged Liam to loosen up. They both would've been much better off if she'd just used one of the pictures he'd brought with him, and she'd sent him on his way. But there was no going back and changing things now. They could only move forward. And that's exactly what she intended to do. The bachelor auction was exactly a week away, and she couldn't afford to have anything go wrong.

Chapter Seven

Feeling foolish for letting her heart control her head, Kate avoided Liam for most of the week. She didn't return his calls.

And he hadn't left a message other than to say, "Please tell her Liam Thayer called."

If it had been important—for instance, if he were calling to back out of the auction—he would've left a message. She certainly would have called him back if it had been something important. Returning an important call would've been the professional thing to do.

If nothing else she prided herself on her professionalism—despite any unfortunate misconceptions brought on by that kiss. They'd both gotten caught up in the moment. However, if someone were to blame, she supposed it could be her. That way there were no expectations. No hurt feelings. No further misunderstandings.

She fully intended to go through with the business

arrangement that they'd made: she would bid on him with the money that he'd donated; he would fulfill his obligation to his boss, and she would get the donations needed for the pediatric surgical wing. Everyone got what they wanted. And she and Liam were both adult enough to not let the kiss ruin it.

Right now she still had a million things to do over the next twenty-four hours. At the moment she was checking off one of the tasks. She and her sister-in-law, Pepper, were at the Dallas/Fort Worth International Airport picking up Maya LeBlanc, who had just flown in from Mont Saint-Michel to promote the expansion of her new international line of chocolates and to serve as the emcee of the bachelor auction.

"It's so wonderful to meet you, Maya," Kate said as she and Pepper helped Maya put her bags in Pepper's black Infiniti SUV. "The chocolate samples you sent are to die for. I don't know if they'll make me fall in love with a man, but I'm definitely in love with Maya's Chocolates."

Maya and Pepper had been good friends for several years. In fact, Pepper swore that Maya had foretold her marriage to Kate's brother, Rob. That's why Pepper had such a special connection to the French woman. Kate had heard so many wonderful things about Maya, she felt as if she already knew her, too.

"Thanks so much for donating the chocolate party favors for the auction and for agreeing to emcee the show," Kate said.

"How cool is it that we have a genuine matchmaker emceeing to boot?" Pepper's voice gushed with pride. After all, it had been Pepper's idea to invite Maya to be the front person for the auction.

A serene smile turned up the corners of Maya's red-painted lips. "You girls are going to make my head swell," she answered in heavily accented English. The contrast of the crimson lipstick against her ivory skin and cascading red curls was striking. What made it even better was that the woman seemed just as beautiful on the inside as she was on the outside.

"These are the touches that will make this event such a great success," Kate added. "I can't thank you enough for taking the time to be here."

"Actually the timing was perfect," she said. "Pepper and Sydney have been so kind to create a public-relations plan for the North American launch of Maya's Chocolates. I can't believe the kindness and generosity of everyone involved with *Catering to Dallas*."

She was right; the timing *was* perfect. *Catering to Dallas* was a reality TV show in its second season, aired nationally on the *Epicurean Traveler Network* which chronicled the inner workings of the local catering company, Celebrations, Inc., which was owned by Pepper and her three partners, A.J., Sydney and Caroline.

When a couple planning to renew their marriage vows had backed out after discovering exactly what being on reality TV involved, the producers had agreed to feature the bachelor auction instead.

Just then Pepper's phone buzzed with a text message. Since she was driving, she picked it up and handed it to Maya, who was riding in the passenger seat. "Would you be a sweetie and see who is texting me, please?"

"Certainly," Maya said, opening the text. "It's from Sarah Cosgrove. Would you like for me to read the text to you?"

"Yes, please," said Pepper.

Sarah was the new Celebrations, Inc., event coordinator. Thanks to the television show and the great reputation the business had built, there were so many events on the books that the girls had been able to hire Sarah full-time to share some of the workload.

"She says, 'Checking in to let you know that I have confirmed the final number of attendees for tomorrow night's auction, and I have arranged for tables to accommodate everyone.'"

Those were two more things that Kate could cross off her list.

"The girl is heaven-sent," said Pepper. "She's an absolute angel. I don't know what we did without her before she came on board. You're just going to love her, Maya. Everybody does."

"I can attest to that," said Kate. "There is no way on earth we would've been able to pull off this event without her."

"Well, honey," said Pepper, glancing in the rearview mirror at Kate, "you just sit back and leave everything to Sarah because she has it all under control. You can enjoy your party and leave the minutia to her."

"I don't know about that," Kate said. The thought of leaving the all-important details in someone else's hands made Kate's eye twitch. She was not a *guest* at this party. She would take a brief break during the auction to fulfill her promise to Liam and bid on him, but she wouldn't be there to enjoy herself. There was too much riding on the evening.

"Well, we'll see about that," said Pepper.

Maya, who was riding shotgun, turned around in her seat and talked to Kate, who was in the backseat. "Are you married, or do you have a special someone in your life?"

Kate laughed. "Me? Oh, no. I'm so busy with work

these days, I don't have time to date, much less time for a *special someone*."

For some odd reason, Liam's face flashed through her mind. She saw him, the way he had looked last Saturday as he had leaned in for the kiss. She blinked away the memory. Thinking of him as anything other than a friend—or better yet, a business acquaintance—was a lost cause.

She sighed despite herself.

Why did he have to be so darned attractive?

He was uptight and unattainable, except when he was leaning in and invading her personal space.

"Pepper, would you mind turning up the air conditioner?" Kate asked. "It's a little warm back here."

"So you are unattached?" Maya said. Her green eyes sparkled. "What an opportunity this auction must be for you."

"Oh, it is. It is exactly the type of project that's a perfect fit for our foundation and my personal goals. We feel fortunate to have the opportunity to give back to our community."

"Yes, it certainly is a good cause, but what I meant was, being young and single, it must be fun to be in the middle of a project with so many good-looking available men. Have you chosen yours yet? It's rare that such an exquisite selection is delivered right to you."

Maya smiled, and for a moment, Kate didn't know what to say. Was she kidding? Kate didn't think so.

Then Maya said, "Give me your hand."

"What?"

Maya reached over the seat, extending her hand to Kate. "I know you might think this is a little crazy, but you do know I'm a matchmaker as well as a chocolatier, remember? I need to see something. Please give me your hand."

Kate saw Pepper watching her in the rearview mirror. "Kate, don't overthink it," she said. "Just do what Maya says."

Kate sensed a conspiracy. Pepper was so happily married to Rob that she made no secret of the fact that she wanted to find a man for Kate, too. For a moment Kate wondered if her sister-in-law had prearranged this with Maya. It had been a fun joke. Up until now. Kate really wasn't in the mood.

However, Kate didn't want to be rude to Maya or embarrass Pepper. What was the harm in playing along?

"I will do it as long as you promise to keep your eyes on the road, missy," she said to Pepper. "I don't want to end up in a ditch."

"Touché," Pepper said. But Kate caught her sister-in-law alternating between watching the road and stealing quick glances in the mirror, no doubt making sure that Kate was, indeed, complying with what Maya was asking.

Kate leaned forward, meeting Maya halfway, and put her hand in Maya's. Holding Kate's hand, the beautiful older woman closed her eyes and didn't make a sound for a good thirty seconds. That was a long, awkward time to be holding hands with a woman she'd just met. But finally Maya gave Kate's fingers a quick squeeze and opened her eyes.

"Just as I thought." She smiled.

"What?" Kate asked, curious to know what this game was all about.

"You've already met your soul mate," she said matter-of-factly, as if she'd told Kate it would rain tomorrow.

"I beg your pardon?" Kate choked on her words. She

was still sitting on the edge of the backseat, and the seat belt was cutting into her collarbone. But that wasn't as important as getting to the bottom of what Maya was talking about.

"You've already met your soul mate," Maya repeated. The woman couldn't have looked any happier if she'd delivered the news that Kate had just won the international lottery—if there was such a thing.

"I don't mean to be rude, but I don't think so. I haven't even had time to go out on a date lately, and the last guy I went out with was definitely—*definitely*—not soul-mate material. I'm sorry to disappoint you, but sadly I haven't even been within a one-hundred-mile radius of my soul mate. I don't even know that I have one."

Maya smiled serenely and listened patiently to Kate, as if she were used to dealing with skeptics.

"Aah, my sweet girl, as the old saying goes, 'There's a lid for every pot.' You may not be aware of it yet, but you have already met him—and recently. I have a strong hunch you met him through the auction. So think about it.... Is there anyone in particular who stands out in your mind?"

Maya's words knocked Kate's breath out of her. Or maybe it was the image of Liam as it crowded its way into her head. For a moment it edged out all other thoughts, until good sense finally reminded her that it was ridiculous to think about Liam Thayer and the words *soul mate* in the same context. The guy had made it very clear that getting involved with anyone was the farthest thing from what he wanted.

Good grief, if he ever did decide he was ready to jump back into the dating pool, Kate felt sorry for any woman who would fall for him. Not only was he emotionally unavailable, but Joy Thayer would be one heck of a hard act to follow. The thought made Kate shudder.

"Aah, so you're thinking of him now."

Kate shook her head. "No, I'm not. I was thinking about one of the more difficult bachelors I've been working with, trying to get everything smoothed out for him so that he feels comfortable participating."

"And you'll bid on him for yourself?" Maya asked.

What the heck? Was the woman a psychic, too? She hadn't told anyone of the deal she'd struck with Liam. How did Maya know? Probably just a lucky guess.

"Yes."

Maya's eyes widened, and Kate could see Pepper peering at her in the rearview mirror again.

"Uhm, how come this is the first I've heard of this?" Pepper asked. "Lucy, I think you have some 'splaining to do."

Kate suppressed a smile. "Eyes on the road, *Ricky*. If you have a wreck, there may not be a bachelor auction."

The thought brought Joy Thayer to mind, and Kate quickly blinked it away. Pepper was a good driver. They would be safe and sound.

"It's not what you think," Kate said. "It's a business arrangement. Do you know Dr. Liam Thayer?"

"I do. He's gorgeous. Don't tell me that *he's* your soul mate. Is he? *Is* he?"

"Why?" Kate asked. "Would you not approve?"

"Hell, yes, I'd approve, but he's a little…" Pepper paused. "How do I say this without ruining it if he does end up being the great love of your life?"

Kate leaned in toward the front seat so that she could better hear Pepper. "Just say it. He's not going to be the great love of my life, as you put it. The only reason I'm bidding on him is because I'm helping him get out of hot water with his boss.

"Liam is a widower with two kids. He says he's not ready to date, but his boss wants all the staff doctors to participate in the auction. You know, it's a teamwork thing. It's not a personal thing. It's a business arrangement. He's making a sizable donation to the auction on the down-low and I'm going to use that money to kiss him."

"You're going to do what?" Pepper shrieked.

Maya's eyes widened as if Kate had just spilled the best secret they'd ever heard.

"I'm going to bid on him," Kate said. "It's really not that big of a deal."

Pepper was gaping at her in the rearview mirror. Kate couldn't see her sister-in-law's mouth, but based on the giddiness in her eyes, Kate knew Pepper's mouth was shaped into an excited O.

"You said you were going to use the money to *kiss* him," Pepper insisted.

"I did not." Kate's cheek's flamed. "I said I was going to bid on him."

"No, you didn't. You said 'kiss.'"

Oh, my gosh, did I say "kiss"? I couldn't have said "kiss." Please, dear God, I didn't say "kiss."

Kate bit her bottom lip to rid herself of the phantom feel of Liam's lips on hers. She shouldn't have told them about bidding. See, it was only causing trouble. She should've kept her mouth shut. And she shouldn't have kissed Liam Thayer.

Wits. She needed to gather her wits, but that was difficult to do with Maya staring at her, scrutinizing her every expression.

Kate turned and gazed out the window to preempt her face from belying her as her tongue had.

"Did I say 'kiss'?" She tried her best to sound blasé. She even gave an indifferent single-shoulder shrug. "If I did, it was probably just a slip."

"A Freudian slip," Pepper said, glee still flowering her voice.

"More like the power of suggestion stemming from Maya's soul-mate comment. Soul mates kiss. I'm definitely not bidding on Dr. Thayer so I can kiss him."

Shut up. Shut up. Shut up. You're just digging yourself in deeper the more you talk.

"Besides, weren't you going to say something before we got off on this dead-end track? Oh, and by the way, you all can't tell anyone about my arrangement with Dr. Thayer. My bidding on him."

"What about your kissing him?" Pepper was only teasing, Kate could tell by the tone of Pepper's voice, but her words made Kate's heart race to rival the time she actually had kissed Liam.

Dear God, she didn't want to care for him. Why, then, was her body reacting the way it was? And why did she have a feeling that Maya was reading her like front-page headlines on the *Dallas Morning News?*

"You're very funny," Kate said. "Don't say a word about any of this. To no one. Now what were you going to say?"

"Well, he's a little *damaged,*" Pepper said.

"Why do you say that?" Maya asked.

Pepper recounted the story of Joy Thayer's fatal accident and how the entire town of Celebration had mourned her loss right alongside Liam and his two daughters.

"That's part of the reason I've agreed to bid on him,"

Kate defended. "So it's not really fair to call him *damaged.* He's simply a man grieving the loss of his wife."

Pepper had exited the highway and was stopped at a red light at the bottom of the off-ramp. She turned around and looked at Kate with large brown eyes. "So what's the rest of the reason you're bidding on him?"

"Green light." Kate nodded toward the front, and Pepper turned back around and eased the car into a left turn. "This guy's heart is completely unavailable. Plus he has two teenage daughters. He's not what I'd call *damaged,* but he does have some baggage, including a failed relationship because apparently someone—some woman here locally—got a little predatory and tried to get her claws in him right after Joy died. He didn't go into details, but he said it didn't end well."

"Kimela Herring!" Pepper shrieked. She'd come to another red light and had turned around again. This time her eyes were wide and brimming over with wanting to tell.

"Who is Kimela Herring?" Kate asked.

"Oh. My. Gosh. She's a disaster. A pushy, overly spray-tanned, anorexic bleach-blonde broad who is an accident waiting to happen. I'm surprised you don't know her but lucky for you that you don't."

"Green light," Kate said, filled with a mixture of unease and curiosity. Once again Pepper turned around and drove on, watching the road, as she told the story of how Kimela Herring, a neighbor of the Thayers, had put the moves on Liam shortly after Joy had passed away.

"I don't know all the details, but the way the story supposedly goes, she was already doing her best to worm her way into his bed at the reception following Joy's funeral. She was very obvious. Didn't even have the decency to wait a while. I know this isn't the Victorian era but seriously. Show some respect."

"Obviously it takes two to have a relationship," Kate said. "We can't necessarily call Liam the victim here."

Pepper made a disgusted noise. "You don't know Kimela Herring. That woman is so transparent that everyone can see her agenda. She's been married *four* times." Pepper held up four fingers. "To be fair, the first husband, a man who was a lot older than she was, passed away and left her quite a bit of money. She supplemented that nest egg with tidy divorce settlements from the other three marriages. Apparently Liam was in her crosshairs to be number five."

"He mentioned that she didn't always have the girls' best interests at heart. Do you know anything about that?" Kate asked.

Pepper shook her head. "I had heard she was trying to ship the daughters off to some kind of a ballet residency program, but that's all I know. I'll do a little reconnaissance and see what I can find out."

If anyone could dig around and not tip her hand, it was Pepper. The woman had a Southern charm that had people spilling national secrets before they realized what they were doing.

Even though Kate knew she shouldn't pry into what had happened between Liam and Kimela, she wanted to know.

Kate watched as downtown Celebration whizzed by in a blur of bricks and awnings, but her gaze picked out Luigi's Italian Kitchen where she'd met Liam for lunch last week.

"He's a good guy even if he is a bit uptight," she volunteered. "He's very protective of his kids. Can't blame him for that."

Pepper sighed. "Sounds like he has a loneliness complex."

"A what?" Kate asked.

"A loneliness complex. It's when someone chooses to be alone."

"Oh, I don't know about that," said Kate. "It's not as if he's choosing loneliness. He's just choosing not to date until after his daughters are out of the house. And since when did you become the resident psychoanalyst?"

"You know me," Pepper said. "I have to try to figure out everyone. Especially if there's a chance they might get close to my sister-in-law."

"Well, don't bank on that," Kate said, but she wasn't sure her friends up front heard her.

"What kind of a doctor is he?" Maya asked, looking up from her phone. She'd been silently reading something since they'd gotten off the highway. Even so, Kate could tell Maya had been listening.

"He's a pediatric hospitalist," Kate said.

"Pardon?" Maya asked.

"He is in charge of pediatrics at Celebration Memorial Hospital," Kate said.

Maya held up her phone, on which she'd called up the bachelor auction's homepage on her internet browser. "I am looking at the auction's website, and I do not see your Liam. His full name is Dr. Liam Thayer, no? How am I missing his photo and biography?"

Kate blanched, suddenly very self-conscious about the confession she had to make. "He's in the auction, but he's not on the website."

"Why not?" Pepper and Maya asked different versions of the question that called for the same answer.

Maya added, "I have the strongest feeling this might turn out to be more than just a business deal."

Kate pretended she didn't hear her, and Maya had the good grace not to push the issue.

"Since I'm bidding on him, I decided—well, *we* decided it would be better to leave him out of the publicity."

That wasn't exactly how the story went, but it was close enough. Liam had asked her if there was a possibility they could leave him off the website. At first she'd said no, but this week she realized it would probably make things easier in the long run. The women who had purchased tickets to the auction and were going to bid had been encouraged to peruse the auction's website. Why drum up business for a bachelor who preferred to fly under the radar?

Or at least that was the story she was telling herself now.

At the start of the week, she couldn't bring herself to look at the pictures of Liam…the ones that were still on her camera phone. As time wore on, her reason for him not appearing on the website had evolved into the version she'd told Pepper and Maya.

And wasn't it true? She couldn't look at the pictures, because she was trying very hard not to fall for a bachelor who preferred to remain unattached.

Chapter Eight

Be careful what you wish for, because you just might get it, Liam thought as he stood in the lobby of the Regency Cypress Plantation on Saturday night, staring at the Bachelor Board.

It featured the mugs of six of his colleagues, but his photo was missing. It was okay. In fact, as far as he was concerned, it was a very good thing. But it was also a very good thing that Rebecca Flannigan, Kate's assistant, had called him on Thursday to fill him in on tonight's drill. Otherwise he might have thought he was off the hook and didn't have to show up at all.

Rebecca had told him when to arrive; she'd suggested what he should wear. She'd even said, "Ms. Macintyre asked me to give you a message that everything is still scheduled to go according to the plan. She will see you Saturday night."

Okay. He got the message. Loud and clear.

And it was underscored when Rebecca—not Kate—emailed him a copy of the night's schedule; he was last on the auction block. He figured Kate had designed it that way so that the bidders would blow their budgets on the bachelors who were up for auction before him, and few, if any, would have money to bid on him. That was a great plan, but it would've been nice if he could've heard it from Kate.

He hadn't been able to reach her this week, and he couldn't help but wonder if it was because of the kiss.

Well, yeah, it was because of the kiss, but he wished he could've had the opportunity to apologize, to tell her they could push the figurative reset button and go on as before.

No harm. No foul.

By this point he figured that he should stop calling. He didn't want to be a nuisance. See, it had been so long since he'd been out in the field that he didn't even know if that was how someone who wasn't interested conveyed the message these days.

The no-message message.

He heard her loud and clear.

Liam made his way into the ballroom. A jazz quartet played music on the stage. Various food stations were set up around the room. He plucked a chocolate truffle off a server's tray—a magical truffle, meant to help him fall in love, the server had said. Liam did his best not to smirk. Instead, he popped the candy into his mouth, went to the bar and ordered a beer. There was no doubt that the chocolate was delicious, but it didn't make him any more eager to walk out on that stage and humiliate himself.

He got his beer, and stood back and watched the preauction cocktails/hors d'oeuvres hour unfold all around him. A chance for the bidders to eat, drink and check out the livestock before they made their final decision on whether or not they wanted to shell out serious money.

Liam might have felt like a piece of meat, if not for the fact that no one except Kate and his colleagues, who were all engaged in conversations at the moment, even knew he would be up for bid.

It was kind of entertaining to observe everyone. Leaning against a vacant high-top table, Liam took in the room, noticing the various women who were crowded around each of the bachelors, making mental bets with himself about who each of his colleagues would end up with. He liked being anonymous, being able to silently survey all the goings-on.

The guys were definitely in their element, like kids in a candy store with more choices than any of them could ever process, much less narrow down so they could select just one. But they didn't have to choose just one, and for a moment, he hoped that each of them got their fill. They were all good guys, each and every one of them. They were single. Why shouldn't they have some fun until the right one came along?

Liam's gaze swept the crowded ballroom. Kate was still nowhere in sight. She had said that the plan was on. For a moment he hoped that she hadn't sent her assistant, Rebecca, in her place.

He watched as a guy did something technical to the TV camera that was set up to tape the auction for that reality show…. What was it called? Something about catering. Liam didn't have a lot of time to watch TV, and the girls didn't watch it. So he couldn't remember the name off the top of his head.

He hoped that the auction being broadcast would

give the extra financial boost to the fund-raiser like Kate was hoping.

His gaze swept the room again. Still no Kate. He wished he knew who Rebecca was…just in case Kate blew him off tonight like she had his phone calls earlier in the week. He supposed, if a random woman bid five thousand dollars on him, that would probably be Kate's assistant. He just needed to relax and go with it. The fund-raiser was almost over and then his life could get back to normal.

"Well, if it isn't Dr. Liam Thayer," purred a sultry voice. "Darlin', it has been far too long."

Liam glanced to his right and his neighbor Kimela Herring was standing there in a low-cut dress that accentuated her pumpkin-tinged tan and other bodily enhancements she was so proud of. She had a flute of champagne in her right hand. Her left hand was stretched out as if she were granting him permission to kiss her bulbous diamond cocktail ring.

Liam opted to give her fingers a polite squeeze. "Hello, Kimela. Why am I not surprised to see you here?"

"You know little ol' me," she said. "I always love a good party and this one is supposed to be hosting only the most handsome eligible men in town. Though, I was shocked to learn that your name was not on the roster. How in the world could that be? An auction of eligible doctors and you're not in the big middle of it? Honey, I almost boycotted on your behalf."

"Well, you can see that I'm here and no worse for the wear."

"Yes, you are here, and you do look fabulous. I am so happy to see that you are not *worse for the wear,* as you put it. Because that would be a terrible thing."

He knew what Kimela was insinuating—that they hadn't said a single word to each other in the past year. Here she was making nice, as if she'd never tried to ship his daughters off to New York City…to that dance program. To hell with that.

At the time they were only eleven years old. Their mother had just died. Liam had still been in a state of shock. That was still the only way he could account for letting this woman worm her way in and wreak such havoc in their lives. He still got angry when he thought of it.

"So, Liam, tell me. Why are you not in this auction? Seems to me that you should be, since you are the head of pediatrics at the hospital. Don't tell me you're still swearing off women."

He thought of Kate. His heart tightened. It was an odd sensation. If it were up to him, he certainly wouldn't swear off *her*. His gaze swept the crowd yet again, but he still didn't see her.

Some people might have taken offense to Kimela's swearing-off-women remark. But Liam had heard that she liked to play rough. That was her way of baiting him, trying to get him to banter. He supposed it was her idea of foreplay—although he wouldn't know since he'd never slept with her.

"Kimela, I've never sworn off women. I'm just waiting for the right one to come along."

Then, by the grace of God, before she could respond, the program started.

"Good evening, everyone. *Bonsoir,* my name is Maya LeBlanc," said the redhead at the podium on the stage. She had a lilting French accent, but her English was impeccable. "I am your mistress of ceremonies for to-night's fun. Ladies, please step back and give the gentlemen some room to make their way backstage. And please don't—how do you say?—*Please, don't squeeze the Charmin.*

"You must give a very big donation to the foundation if you wish to do that." A polite bubble of laughter rippled through the room. "And on that note I do hope everyone brought their checkbooks and will be very generous to help us build the pediatric surgical wing at Celebration Memorial Hospital.

"I know everyone is excited to begin. No? Are you excited? If you are, please put your hands together and let our handsome bachelors know how much you appreciate them. Please remember that, since there are only seven bachelors to win this evening, we still have the silent auction happening in the lobby. It will close in ten minutes.

"Tonight you may purchase tickets to the fund-raising completion celebration. If you are one of the lucky ladies with the winning bid tonight, you and your bachelor will also win a ticket to the fund-raising completion celebration. So it is as if you will win two dates tonight. At this time we need all participating bachelors backstage now, please."

"What?" said Kimela. "She said *seven* bachelors will be auctioned off tonight. But there are only six doctors listed in the program. I wonder if she made a mistake? Or are you a surprise guest?"

Liam shrugged. Why was it that this woman, who was possibly one of the most unperceptive people he'd ever met, always seemed to pick up on the things that he hoped would go over her head? He could club her with something obvious, trying to drive home a point, and it would completely escape her. No, Kimela Herring was not one to intuit subtle hints, or maybe she just didn't care when an intimation went contrary to that on which she'd set her steel-trap mind.

"I need to go, Kimela," Liam said. "And you should probably go stake your claim so you don't miss out on casting a winning bid. Have fun."

"Where are you sitting?" she asked. "If you don't have a table, we can certainly make room for you at ours."

"I appreciate the offer, but I have a previous commitment."

As the words escaped his mouth, he finally spied Kate in the crowd. She looked stunning in a pink sparkly little number that hugged her curves in all the right places. She seemed to glow, and he wondered how he'd missed her until now. He knew she saw him too, because she didn't break eye contact with him as she turned and whispered something to the blonde who was with her. The friend did a not-so-subtle turn-and-look, then said something to Kate.

As Kate and her friend were looking his way, Kimela chose that precise moment to angle herself in front of him, reach up with a possessive hand and pluck a piece of lint off his lapel. She finished the show by brushing something off his shoulder.

He felt her long coral-colored nails scrape his suit fabric. The talons looked like weapons, as if they could've left a mark if she chose to do so. Before Liam could take a step away from Kimela, a group of people passed in front of him, blocking his line of vision to Kate. By the time they'd moved out of the way, Liam had lost sight of her.

He knew there was no easier way to extract himself than to just walk away. So he did what he had to do.

"Excuse me," he said, and turned and walked away.

He felt Kimela's gaze on him. So he went to the bar to kill time until he was sure she wasn't watching him anymore.

"There you are," said Rebecca. "I've been looking all over the place for you. You need to come backstage right now. Everyone is lining up."

As he started to follow Rebecca, who was already ten steps ahead of him, Kimela crossed in front of him. She waved and gave him a knowing smile.

"Liam, come on," Rebecca motioned from the stage entrance.

"I think they need you backstage," Kimela said. Liam had a sinking feeling he'd just witnessed the harbinger of doom.

"Is he here with her?" Pepper hissed.

Kate craned her neck, trying to see around a knot of people who were blocking their view.

"Why would he come to an event like this with a date?" Kate challenged. "Let's go sit down at our table. I don't want Liam to see us gawking at him."

Pepper told her husband, Rob, where they were going, then followed Kate.

"I can't imagine that he would bring her," said Pepper. "I did a little detective work and found out what Kimela did to make Liam so angry."

"What?" Kate asked.

"I have a friend who is on the board at the New School of Ballet with Kimela. She told me that Kimela pulled some strings to get the girls a place with the Randolph Ballet school's residential program in New York."

"What's wrong with that?" Kate glanced around to make sure no one was listening in on their talk. "It sounds like every little ballerina's dream."

"One would think, right?" Pepper leaned in closer and whispered, "Well, rumor has it that one of the daughters made it into the program on her own merit, but the other didn't. The strings Kimela pulled were to get the other daughter a residency. I don't know exactly what happened after all this. But obviously neither girl ended up moving to New York, and he and Kimela ended up on the outs."

"Well, they are thirteen years old now, and so they were likely only eleven or twelve then," Kate said. "That's a little young to pack up and move to the big city on their own."

"I guess you could look at it like a boarding school."

"Where you study ballet rather than reading, writing and arithmetic. Given how short-lived a ballerina's career is, I can't say I'd be overly enthusiastic about my girls wanting to put all their eggs into that basket."

"You do know that Joy used to be a ballerina, don't you?" asked Pepper. "Apparently, she was quite good but ended up cashing it all in to stay with Liam. Maybe she had been grooming the girls to realize the dream she gave up for marriage and a family. She and Kimela were good friends. I wonder if Kimela was just trying to carry out Joy's wishes?"

Kate shrugged, more so to ward off the uneasy feeling that always seemed to engulf her when Joy's name came up. The woman seemed to get more and more perfect every time someone mentioned her.

"Enough about that," Pepper said. "A better question is why are you not over there talking to the gorgeous Dr. Thayer? Or better yet, why didn't he pick you up and bring you here tonight? That way we wouldn't be speculating about what he's doing with Kimela."

Why not? If the truth be known, after that kiss, Kate

had been scared out of her wits. She'd felt something the likes of which she'd never felt before, and suddenly she had a taste of what it just might feel like to be the person in the relationship who cared the most. And after all, she and Liam didn't even have anything close to a relationship.

His kiss had rendered her so vulnerable that the only thing she'd been able to do was run and hide out all week like a scared rabbit. As she took a seat at the table, she felt foolish. If Maya hadn't just called everyone to order, she might have gone over to Liam and said something, but by the time the crowd had cleared, she saw Kimela standing alone, with Liam nowhere in sight.

After the auction was over and the dust had settled, she'd apologize to him for being so scarce this week.

Her brother joined them at the table. Before he sat down, he leaned in and planted a quick kiss on Pepper's lips. Kate looked away and smiled, though hit by a sudden, strange stitch of envy for what Rob and Pepper had. What was that?

She wasn't jealous of her brother and sister-in-law. How could she be *jealous?* Just because she wasn't in the market for a relationship didn't mean she wasn't thrilled that her brother had found someone as wonderful as Pepper. Pepper made Rob happy. In fact, Kate wasn't sure if she'd *ever* seen her brother this relaxed and content before.

Once more, her gaze searched the crowded room for Liam. She didn't find him. He must be backstage with the others. Kimela was still standing alone.

Kate was suddenly happy that she'd made the decision to not include Liam in the program because there was something kind of intimate about being the only one who was planning on bidding on him.

A knot formed in the pit of her stomach, reminding her that the kiss they'd shared the other day had been a mistake. That tonight was all about business, just an agreement they'd made. She was happy to be single, answering to and worrying about no one other than herself. Her life was far better than one complicated by romantic entanglements.

Maya made several more humorous remarks.

"She's good," Pepper said. "Who knew? This will be a fabulous spot for the TV show."

Since Celebrations, Inc., had provided the food and the event coordination, they had taped the preparation of the auction. It had been difficult for Kate to sit back and let event coordinator Sarah Cosgrove handle tonight's logistics, but Kate had. And Sarah had done a beautiful job.

Kate had arrived an hour before the guests were set to turn up to make sure everything was in place. And it was. The plantation's ballroom, which had good bones anyway with its stained-glass windows, hardwood floors and gleaming brass fixtures, looked beautiful decorated with strands of small white lights strung across its expanse. The stage was adorned with flowers and topiaries. Food tables with delectable selections were set up at various stations around the room.

The work was done. All Kate had to do was walk Maya through the program. Maya, the fabulous, was one step ahead of her. She'd already written herself an informal script.

With Pepper on her heels insisting that Kate enjoy the evening, Kate backed off and let the others do their jobs. Relaxing, however, was a completely different story.

She wouldn't be able to—not in the formfitting, pink-beaded bandage cocktail dress she was wearing—and certainly not until she'd fulfilled her promise to Liam Thayer, and he was bought and paid for.

The festivities got underway. They'd allotted fifteen minutes per bachelor with a break in between each to announce the winners of the silent auction items.

It was fun to watch the occasional bidding war erupt. Some of the women could be downright competitive. Case in point was when Kimela Herring, who was seated behind Kate a couple tables to the right, had gotten into a heated bidding war with two women over Quinn Vogler, the hospital's staff orthopedist. Quinn was the last person before Liam would take the stage.

Kimela was a formidable opponent. In other words, she intended to win. She kept raising her paddle until the bid reached $7,500 and her rival finally gave up.

Kate was happy about the high bid for a few reasons: *obviously,* because it meant more money for the hospital; and *selfishly,* because she hoped that meant that Kimela had spent her bachelor auction budget. Maybe that was proof that Liam hadn't told her that he was going to be a *surprise* add-on to close out the event.

Finally the moment of truth had arrived.

"Ladies, I have good news for those of you who were not fortunate enough to win one of the six fabulous men who have so graciously appeared on this stage. We have one more bachelor for your consideration. Let us all please welcome Dr. Liam Thayer to the stage."

As Liam walked out onto the stage, a round of applause sounded. "Ladies, Dr. Thayer is head of pediatrics at Celebration Memorial Hospital. He is six foot four. He has brown hair and blue eyes. His interests are kayaking, wine tasting and sports."

When Liam's gaze snared Kate's, nerves rolled through her stomach. It was as if he'd zeroed right in on her. Of course backstage he might have been able to see the audience. So she wouldn't allow herself to make too big of a deal over it.

He walked up to Maya at the podium.

"Hello, handsome," she said. Someone in the audience whistled. Kate wished she'd asked Maya to go a little more low-key when she presented Liam. However, since they were already at the hall when Kate had been walking Maya through the last-minute details, Kate didn't want to say too much for fear that someone might overhear her. Besides, as intuitive as Maya seemed to portray herself, Kate didn't think she needed to push the issue.

"Are you the kind of guy who likes to surprise women?" she asked. "Because you're the evening's big surprise. You're not listed in the program. The ladies out there didn't know you'd be here tonight. Can you tell us why?"

Kate shook her head as discreetly as she could, hoping Maya would see her and curtail that line of questioning.

"I guess I do like to surprise people, Maya. Isn't life sometimes one big surprise? That's what keeps life interesting."

The audience applauded wildly.

"Well, there you go," Maya said. "Ladies, if you like surprises, then cast a bid for a mystery date with Dr. Liam Thayer, the man who is full of surprises. I'll open the bidding at five hundred dollars. Do I hear five hundred dollars for Dr. Thayer?"

Kate was so relieved and impressed by the way Liam handled himself; he seemed so completely unfazed by

Maya's questions, it almost seemed planned. Just as she was about to hold up her placard, Maya pointed to someone to the right of Kate and said, "Five hundred dollars, right here, do I hear six hundred?"

Kate's hand shot up.

Maya pointed to her. "Six hundred right here. Do I hear seven?"

The woman to her right bid again. This time Kate got a look at the competition. Kimela Herring. Kate and Pepper exchanged a look.

"Oh, for God's sake," Kate muttered under her breath. The woman had already won the date with Quinn Vogler. Why did she have to be so greedy? Especially when it was clear that Liam had no interest in her.

Or did he?

Of course he didn't. He'd made that perfectly clear. Just because he was talking to her before the auction didn't mean anything other than he was being polite. Still, how much money did one woman have to purchase dates? Kate decided she would put an end to this right now.

When Maya raised the bid to eight hundred, Kate raised her placard and said, "Fifteen hundred dollars."

The audience gasped.

Maya smiled and pointed to Kate. "Fifteen hundred dollars right here. Do I hear sixteen hundred?"

The room was so silent Kate was afraid people could hear her shallow breathing and the staccato beat of her heart.

"Fifteen hundred dollars, going once…going twice—"

"Three thousand dollars," said Kimela.

Once again the audience gasped. So did Kate. Was the woman kidding? Was she desperate? Kate and Liam had joked about a bidding war, but they hadn't talked about what to do in case someone drove the price above the allotted five thousand dollars. Until now it would've seemed like a ridiculous discussion.

She looked at Liam, who was staring at her, a broad smile plastered on his face. As if he could do anything else with all eyes on him. For lack of a better idea, Kate, trying to be as subtle as she could, leaned her elbow on the table and propped her chin on her fist. This allowed her to make a subtle thumbs-up sign, and then rotate her fist to make a thumbs-down sign. Hoping and praying that no one was watching her, she flashed her eyes at Liam and repeated the signal.

He gave the faintest of nods at what she was sure was the thumbs-up, which she interpreted to mean he wanted her to continue bidding. Of course. He didn't want to get stuck with Kimela.

"Do I hear thirty-one hundred?" Maya asked in Kate's direction. Now all stares were on her. She had to bid or fold. If she and Liam made another signal, everyone would see. Or she would look like she had some kind of nervous tic.

"Going once…" Maya said.

Kate held up her paddle. The audience cheered. It reminded her of the scene in the movie *It's A Wonderful Life,* when George Bailey and Mary Hatch are dancing at the school dance, and every time they edged closer to the rim of the swimming pool, the crowd would applaud with more and more gusto, until finally they fell in. Good lord. If she fell in this pool, she feared she might drown.

Maya looked back over in Kimela's direction, but before she could raise the bid, the annoying woman held up her placard and said, "Five thousand dollars."

Was she out of her mind?

Obviously so.

As the crowd hooted and hollered, Kate stole a glance at Liam, who gave a short but frantic shake of his head. Which meant…"don't throw me to the wolf"? Or don't bid any higher?

His expression could've meant either.…

Oh, they really should've discussed this.

Well, this was her lame-brained scheme and she had promised him that she wouldn't throw him to the wolves. Even if she had to cover the excess of the amount of his check, she would do it. She cast a side-long glance at Kimela, who was reveling in the attention she was getting.

How in the world had Liam gotten messed up with the likes of her in her low-cut neckline with her fake spray tan? It wasn't even a good spray tan. You'd think that someone with this kind of money to blow could afford something that looked more natural. Maybe she didn't know the difference, bless her heart.

Right. That woman knew exactly what she was doing. And there was no way Kate was going to let her get her hands on Liam again.

Kimela Herring might be competitive, but the Great Pumpkin hadn't seen anything like Kate Macintyre when she was on a mission.

Ten thousand dollars later, Kimela conceded.

Coincidentally—or not—her withdrawal from the race coincided with Pepper excusing herself to go to the bathroom. At first Kate thought it was an odd time for her sister-in-law to get up and leave. However, on the way she stopped by Kimela's table and whispered something in the woman's ear. Whatever she said must've been particularly effective because that's when Kimela retired her paddle, and Maya had pronounced Kate the winner.

Amid the roar of the crowd, reality, cold and prickly, began to settle in around Kate. She had just bid ten thousand dollars to win Liam his freedom.

Ten. Thousand. Dollars.

It was a good thing she was sitting, because she couldn't feel her legs.

Ten thousand dollars.

Oh, dear God. What the heck had she just done?

Chapter Nine

They were calling him the Ten-Thousand-Dollar Man. They had nicknamed him that even before he was able to make his way to Kate in the sea of well-wishers.

Him being auctioned off for that much money had whipped the crowd into a frenzy, and he was doing his best to act flattered and humbled that someone would spend ten thousand dollars for a date with him.

The burning question was: Where was he going to take Kate? What exactly did a ten-thousand-dollar date consist of?

"It's all for charity," he managed to say off the top of his head.

"Dr. Thayer, I'm Bia Anderson, managing editor of the *Dallas Journal of Business and Development.* I'm covering the auction tonight for the paper. Not to be a skeptic, but since your name wasn't in the program or any of the preauction material, and you are the head of the department which will benefit from this fundraiser…was this a setup?"

He hadn't counted on speaking to the press. "Excuse me?" he asked, pretending not to understand her question. Several people who had been trying to get his attention had heard Bia's question and had stopped to listen to his answer.

"I'm sorry to be a skeptic," she said. "But that was a lot of money. And the woman with the winning bid… her name is Kate Macintyre. She runs the foundation, doesn't she?"

"It is a lot of money," he answered. "And it's for a great cause. I can assure you that everything is on the up-and-up. Kate Macintyre will get her date. The new pediatric surgical wing will benefit from the money. I'm sorry to poke holes in your conspiracy theory."

Bia frowned. "Well, then, where are you taking her? That was another thing that led to me thinking that this was…"

"A setup?" Liam answered. He smiled his most charming smile. "Ms. Anderson, Kate bought herself a ten-thousand-dollar surprise. I can assure you that she will be surprised. But don't you think it would spoil everything if I told you what I had in mind before I told Kate? That would defeat the purpose of the surprise, wouldn't it?"

Bia nodded, conceding, even though her expression gave away that she still wasn't buying Liam's explanation.

"If you'll excuse me," he said, "I need to do the polite thing and find my future date."

"Of course," said the reporter.

As Liam walked away, she said, "But you will let me do a follow-up story, won't you? After the big event? Everyone will be dying to know where the Ten-Thousand-Dollar Man takes his date."

"Let me talk to Kate and see what she has to say about a follow-up."

And did he ever intend to talk to Kate. Bia Anderson had no idea. Funny, though, he wasn't mad at Kate. She'd obviously done what she had thought was for the best. Even though he had no idea how she could've misread his signs. He'd clearly been giving her the signal to stop.

Or at least he had thought he'd been clear about it. But it was over now. Kate had done her best. He'd agreed to the plan. There was nothing more to discuss. The only thing he'd do differently next time is to make sure there wasn't a next time. He would never let his colleagues talk him into doing something he didn't want to do. That was the lesson learned from this night.

People slapped him on the back and congratulated him as he finally made his way through the crowd to Kate.

The people applauded, camera flashes went off. When Kate turned around and saw him, her cheeks flushed the prettiest shade of pink.

The crowd chanted, "Kiss! Kiss! Kiss!"

Someone gave Kate a gentle shove toward Liam, and she landed in his arms with an *umph*. She buried her head in his chest, apparently in no hurry to move away. So he put his arms around her and just held her. As they embraced, he tried not to notice how perfectly they fit together.

"I am so sorry, Liam," she whispered. "I guess I got a little carried away when Kimela started driving up the bid. This got out of control, and I take full responsibility. I will pay the five thousand dollars that I bid over and above what you gave me to work with."

"No, you won't," he whispered. "At least you showed Kimela she can't have everything she wants."

"Yes, but at what cost?"

"Don't worry about it," he said. "It's done, and there's nothing we can do about it now."

She pulled back and looked at him with wide eyes. The color that had flushed her cheeks earlier was gone now, and she looked a little pale and panicked. He worried that he might have sounded a little too harsh.

"You do know that everyone is watching us, don't you?" he whispered over the excited din in the ballroom. "Keep smiling. Otherwise, people will think you're having buyer's remorse."

She forced a smile that didn't quite reach her eyes. "I am," she whispered. Her face was so serious. "Why didn't you signal me to stop bidding?"

"Keep smiling," he urged again. "I did signal you. Like this." He gave a quick jerk of his head.

"Okay, to me that says *keep* bidding," she said.

"I meant *stop* bidding," Liam said.

Kate groaned. "We should've thought ahead. I should've seen this coming. We should've established signals. Or maybe I should've just let Kimela win. I'm sorry, Liam. I'm so sorry."

"Hey, keep smiling," he whispered, careful to soften his tone. He was surprised by how protective he felt over her. She looked so fragile, and he didn't want her to feel bad about this. Ten thousand dollars be damned. He'd think about the ramifications of that later. For now he wanted to see a genuine smile on Kate's face. Because until this moment, he hadn't realized how warm and calm her smile made him feel.

"There's nothing to be sorry about," he answered. "I'm glad you didn't let Kimela win."

She sighed in a way that sounded as if her very soul had deflated. "But ten thousand dollars? That's just… It's just outrageous. Why do you—"

She clamped her mouth shut as if she refused to let out the rest of the question.

"What?" he asked.

She shook her head.

He leaned in with the intention of making sure no one overheard what he was about to say. But the proximity and the scent of her—floral and fresh—took over his senses and made him breathe in deeply. It transported him back to that day in her office when he'd kissed her. He had the overwhelming urge to taste her lips again, so he said the one thing that could bring him back to center.

"Are you wondering why I don't want to see Kimela?"

Kate nodded.

Liam glanced around to make sure no one was listening in on their conversation. The crowd seemed to be dissipating and the *Catering to Dallas* crew seemed to have gotten all the footage it needed. Even so, he kept his voice at a whisper. "It's because she doesn't listen. I told her numerous times that I couldn't get involved, but she wouldn't hear me. She kept manipulating the situation. I guess she thought she could wear me down. The situation wasn't good for either one of us. Right now, my kids have to come first. She didn't understand that."

Kate nodded. "I guess she's a woman who goes after what she wants."

Liam's admission seemed to have lightened Kate's mood.

"I don't know about that. Maybe it's more apt to say she wants what she thinks she can't have. But changing the subject to a much better note, you look beautiful tonight. I like your dress."

"Thank you," she said. "You dress up pretty well yourself. I didn't think you owned anything else besides a lab coat. The tux is a nice change."

"Maybe I'll wear it on our ten-thousand-dollar date everyone is expecting me to take you on."

"Very funny. Don't even joke."

"I'm not joking. That reporter from the *Dallas Journal of Business and Development* asked if she could do a follow-up story on our date."

"And I hope you told her no."

"Not exactly."

"What does that mean?" Kate asked.

"It means when she asked where I was taking you, I told her, since the date was a surprise, I couldn't tell her before I told you. Since we're the talk of this auction, there will be a date and it will be a ten-thousand-dollar date."

Kate grimaced.

"As for a follow-up story, I said I had to check with you first."

Kate laughed with relief on her face, then leaned in to whisper, "Thank you for that."

He wanted to pull her back into his arms, to shelter her from the circus of curious onlookers. Instead, he reached up and brushed a strand of hair off her forehead, remembering the feel of her lips on his.

"So first there was a fake auction bid," Kate began. "Now there's going to be a fake date. Why do I feel like this is a cautionary tale about the perils of lying? One lie forces you to tell another and then another."

"I see what you mean," he said. "If we're not careful, we may end up having to get married."

Kate's eyes flew wide open. "Excuse me?"

Liam shook his head. "And that sounded wrong on so many levels, didn't it?"

"On so many I can't even count them. And for the record, there are certain things I won't pay for."

Right about now Liam would've paid just about any price for one more long, unhurried taste of her lips, and the chance to explore that area where her jaw met her neck. He knew if he did, the scorching sexual magnetism that drew him to her wouldn't let him stop there—

"What are you two lovebirds doing huddled over here together?" asked Pepper.

"Just discussing the terms of our date," Liam said.

"Ah, the ten-thousand-dollar date. Everyone in Celebration is holding their breaths to see where you go from here."

For the first time in a very long time, Liam was wondering the same thing.

As the crowd began to dissipate and people had finally pulled Liam away, offering the Ten-Thousand-Dollar Man congratulatory backslaps and high fives, the reality of what Kate had done began to sink in.

What the heck got into me? she wondered as she stood amid the knot of stragglers still left in the ballroom.

Five thousand dollars above and beyond what Liam had agreed to?

Had she lost her mind? What had driven her to do such a thing? Was she truly trying to save Liam, or had her temporary lapse of reason been goaded by a more selfish motive?

While she was all about charitable giving, she was sure that wasn't what motivated Kimela Herring. Kate didn't have that kind of disposable money lying around to spend on a date with a gorgeous man. But it was too late to second-guess herself now. She'd already committed, and it was time to pay the piper.

And Liam had been so good about it. So understanding. Well, of course he would be understanding since she'd offered to pay what she'd bid over and above his budget. He may have said no, that he wouldn't allow her to pay, but it was only the polite thing to do.

She watched Liam as he talked to Cullen Dunlevy. Kate didn't know when she'd seen a smile that big on the chief of staff's face. Liam was obviously out of the doghouse. Kate was happy she could help him.

It truly had been a win-win situation for all involved tonight—well, maybe not her bank account. But Liam was back in the chief's good graces, and on first accounting, the auction had met its goal.

"Why so glum?" Maya asked. "You should be very happy. You caught the big fish of the night."

Kate narrowed her eyes at her friend. "Maya, you know what the situation is all about. I can hardly say I won. Please make sure no one ever turns me loose in Las Vegas. I think I might have a real gambling problem."

"Mon amie," said Maya. "I don't believe that gambling is your problem. I believe it is love."

Kate bristled. "No, Maya. Not a chance. I realize you're a hopeless romantic. It's one of the hazards of your job as a matchmaker. But neither Liam nor I are in the market for...love."

"Honey, he is the one," Maya said. "Before I met him and observed the two of you together, I couldn't be sure. I had a feeling, but I could not be certain. Now I am certain. Soon you will be, too. This date will be the time that will help you realize it."

The skeptic inside Kate warred with and won out over the glimmer of hope that Maya was right, that Liam Thayer was her soul mate. This was a business arrangement and nothing more.

Even if they did go through with the bogus date—all for show—that's where it would end. Because Liam Thayer had made it perfectly clear that he wasn't interested in anything long-term.

And there was no way Kate would ever allow herself to fall for a man who was emotionally unavailable. She refused to render herself so vulnerable as to repeat her father's mistake by falling in love with someone whose heart belonged to another.

"Do you know who that woman was —the one Liam was talking to after the auction before he made his way over here to be with you?" Maya asked.

"There were several women," Kate said. "Remember, he's the big fish tonight. Can you be more specific?"

"The petite woman with curly auburn hair. She is a member of the press. Ah, she gave me her card. She wants to interview me next week. Wait a moment. Let me get the business card she gave me."

Maya fished the card out of her pocketbook and read the name printed on it. "Bia Anderson?"

"Yes, Bia. She's the managing editor of a local publication," Kate said. "Nice woman. She was asking the usual questions and wants to do a follow-up story after we have our date. That's assuming there will be a date."

"Of course you will have a date," Maya said. "It will be the beginning of a very happy life together for the two of you."

Kate scoffed, but Maya didn't give her time to protest.

"Bia looks so very familiar. I feel as if I've met her

before, but I can't quite place her. It's the strangest feeling."

"We're only acquaintances," Kate asked. "I've met her a few times, but only briefly and in passing. I don't know that much about her. Did you talk to her?"

"Pepper introduced me to her, and then she asked to set up an interview next week."

"Ah, that reminds me," said Kate. "Pepper's colleague Caroline Coopersmith probably knows her better than all of us. Bia works for Caroline's husband, Drew, at the newspaper. Drew is the editor in chief. We could ask Caroline about her."

Maya waved a hand. "Thank you, but, no. I'll talk to Bia next week when we meet for the interview. Maybe then we can get to the bottom of it. Now here comes your man. I will leave you two alone to talk about your future."

Kate sighed, but before she could protest, the Ten-Thousand-Dollar Man was standing in front of her. *Her* Ten-Thousand-Dollar Man…at least for all intents and purposes.

"What a night, huh?" he said, a sexy smile tilting up the corners of his mouth.

"You can say that again."

"I'm heading out now," he said. "I need to get home to the girls. But I wanted to see if I could give you a lift home."

The girls. He really was a good father, always putting his daughters first. She remembered what Pepper had said earlier about how he'd gotten mad at Kimela for trying to come between him and his daughters. She didn't blame him for not wanting to send the girls away.

In fact, she admired him for doing the right thing and keeping them home, raising them on his own.

"I appreciate it, Liam," she said. "But I have my car."

"Well, good night, then."

His tone was so formal, for a split second she feared he might try to shake her hand. But he didn't. He reached out and gathered her in his arms. The heat that sparked from the body-to-body contact made her tingle. Her whole being filled with an almost overwhelming desire to kiss him again, the way they'd kissed in her office.

His lips moved to her ear, but that's where they stopped. "I'll call you so we can figure out this ten-thousand-dollar date."

His breath was hot in her ear, and he smelled wonderful—something green, with a hint of brandy and peppermint. She breathed him in, trying not to melt in his arms. Good thing she didn't, because he let go, and she had to find her balance as she watched him walk away. When he got to the door, he turned around and smiled at her, leaving her with the feeling that tonight she'd bought herself a heck of a lot more than she'd bargained for.

It was after midnight when Liam got home, but as he pulled into the driveway, he could see that the lights in his daughters' bedroom were still ablaze. Since he knew he was going to be out and Rosalinda had agreed to stay with them, he'd allowed each of the girls to have one friend sleep over tonight.

He was exhausted, and he'd hoped that they would be in bed and asleep by now, but given that they were teenage girls, he knew that was a pipe dream. Still, at least their friends would distract them enough to keep

Calee and Amanda from peppering him with questions. If he were lucky, maybe he'd be able to see Rosie to her car and then get away with a quick hello and good-night to the girls before turning in.

He lowered the garage door and let himself in the kitchen door only to find four eager young girls waiting for him. They squealed and hooted when they saw him. Calee launched herself at him, wrapping her flannel-pajama-clad arms and legs around him like a spider monkey. The force of the impact sent him staggering back a few steps. She may have been tiny, but she was a strong little thing. It didn't help that the others were making so much noise that Liam was afraid they might wake up the entire neighborhood.

The last thing he needed was for Kimela to have an excuse to come over and ring the doorbell at this hour. But Rosie—and thank God for Rosie—beat him to the noise control.

"Girls, girls, inside voices, please!" she said.

"You won, Daddy! You won!" Calee hollered.

"Shh...." Liam managed to work an arm free and press a finger to his lips. Calee was still hanging off him, but they all did bring the noise level down several decibels. "What do you mean, *I won?* Did that guy from Publishers Clearing House sweepstakes come by with the balloons and the big check?"

The comment silenced them all the way and for a few beats the four girls looked blankly at each other.

"Is he from the bachelor auction?" asked Calee. "Because if he is, he hasn't come yet. He was probably waiting until you got home. But we already know you won. Ashley Berg's big sister was tweeting live from the auction as everything happened, and we already know you were the bachelor who raised the most money."

"Everyone is calling you the Ten-Thousand-Dollar Man," said Amanda in an unusually assertive manner.

So they'd heard that part, too? It was amazing how fast news traveled. The wonders of social media never ceased to amaze him.

"Ha, ha, ha, take that, Lacy Vogler. You don't have the hottest dad in town! We do!"

The girls resumed their squealing and suddenly Liam had a taste of how that boy band—One Direction, which his girls loved so much—must feel when they were cornered by a group of overexcited teenage fans. Liam couldn't help but smile. He didn't want the girls to hold this over Lacy Vogler's head—and he would make sure he talked to them about that—but he was happy he had made his daughters proud.

"*Ay, mis niñas,* please lower your voices." Rosie put her hands over her ears. "I am going to go deaf from all this noise."

"Girls, please do as Rosie asked and bring it down a bit," he said. "It was a very good night tonight for the fund-raiser. It brought in a lot of money for the pediatric surgical wing."

"And most of it was because of the ten thousand dollars bid on you, Dr. Thayer," said the girls' friend Jane.

"Well, I wouldn't go that far," said Liam. "Really, ten thousand dollars is a small amount when you look at the big picture. This project has cost millions."

It was true. On the one hand, ten thousand dollars was a big chunk of change out of his own bank account. In fact, he was going to have to move around some investments to get the money to cover the amount, because Kate wasn't paying a single dime of it.

He let the thought resonate within him for a moment and realized that not only did he not mind, he was looking forward to his date with Kate. It would be their little secret that they'd done this bachelor auction in reverse. He fully intended to enjoy his ten-thousand-dollar date.

Chapter Ten

"It sounds like *someone* had a great weekend," said Rebecca Flannigan, the Macintyre Family Foundation's office manager and Kate's assistant, as Kate stepped out of the elevator early Monday morning.

"I guess good news travels fast," said Kate.

"I'll say. You and Dr. Dreamy are the talk of the town. Where are you going on your date?"

"We'll see," she said. "Won't we?"

As Rebecca nodded, Kate made her way back to her office. Rebecca's question sort of felt like a moment of truth. Since so many people were paying attention to the *big date,* Kate knew she couldn't keep insisting there wasn't going to be one. If the truth be told, she wouldn't mind spending time with Liam. She just didn't want him to feel obligated.

The whole reason she'd come up with this crazy scheme in the first place was to get him out of the post-auction date. Now all she'd managed to do was focus a bright spotlight on it.

But yesterday afternoon, after all the excitement and mayhem of the evening before was beginning to settle, she'd received a voice mail message from Liam. He'd said, *I know you're exhausted after pulling off such a successful event. And congratulations, by the way. I don't want to keep you. But I do want you to know that I'm looking forward to our big date. Let me plan some things, and I'll call you in a couple days so that we can get something on the books.*

Even the small gesture of his phone call warmed her from the inside out and softened her toward the idea. He hadn't sounded mad or resentful of the attention or the final amount of the bid. That was enough to let her daydream for a moment about what it might be like to spend one glorious night alone with him. One night where it was just them—no talk of auctions or grand plans to pacify the hospital's chief of staff. No crazy women like Kimela or ghosts from the past casting a shadow over the evening. Just two friends enjoying a night alone together.... Of course there was the matter of the kiss. But all she had to do was remind herself that Liam Thayer was not emotionally available. That was better than a cold shower.

Or so she told herself.

Kate had no more than settled herself at her desk and turned on her computer when Rebecca called to let her know that a delivery had arrived for her.

"Can you sign for it?" Kate asked.

"No. I already tried. They won't let me. In fact, you might want to bring your identification. He says he'll need to see it."

Identification? That's strange. What could it be? "Thanks, Rebecca. I'll be right out."

She grabbed her license and made her way back to the lobby, where she saw a guy from a courier service holding an envelope. "Good morning," he said. "Ms. Macintyre?"

"Yes, good morning." She handed him her driver's license before he even had a chance to ask for it.

"Sign right here, please." He handed her the clipboard and a pen. After Kate complied, he handed her the envelope and said, "Thanks so much. Have a great day."

Kate looked at the manila envelope. There was no return address or other markings that indicated who it was from. She opened it and pulled out a folded card with a note typed on its face.

Because you and Dr. Thayer make the perfect couple, this check is to cover the amount of your bidding fees. Congratulations and enjoy your date.

When Kate flipped open the card and saw a cashier's check for ten thousand dollars made out to the Macintyre Family Foundation, her heart began to thud in her chest.

There was no name on the check other than the bank that had issued it. She flipped back to the note; it was unsigned and the delivery envelope contained no return address.

"Is everything okay?" asked Rebecca.

Kate looked up and saw the woman staring at her.

"Yes," Kate answered. "Everything is fine. I'm just not sure who sent this."

The elevator dinged its arrival and before the courier

could get on, Kate hollered, "Excuse me. Do you have any idea who asked you to deliver this?"

The guy reached out and held the elevator doors open, then glanced at his clipboard. "I picked it up from the bank. That's who hired me to drop it off."

"Do you have a name from anyone at the bank?" Kate asked.

"No, I'm sorry. It just says here Celebration Bank. Wish I could be of more help."

"So do I," Kate returned. "Have a nice day."

"You, too." With that the elevator doors shut and Kate was left holding a large check from an anonymous donor.

"What is it?" Rebecca asked.

"A rather sizable donation to the pediatric surgical wing sent by an anonymous donor."

"A mystery donor," said Rebecca. "That's so cool."

Kate nodded, and for the second time that day, she made the trek back to her office where she fully intended to make several phone calls. She was already composing a list of potential people who might have gone to the generous trouble to do this: Liam; Pepper and Rob; Kimela?

Fat chance it was Kimela, based on the not-so-glowing report that Pepper had provided. The woman may have had money to blow on handsome bachelors, but she wasn't the sort to buy someone else a date. Especially one that she'd tried so hard to win.

But really, who else would've sent the check?

When she was back in her office, she called her brother.

"Rob Macintyre," he said in his deep, brusque business voice.

"Rob, it's Kate. Did you and Pepper make a rather

sizable donation to the foundation and have it couriered over a few moments ago?"

"Well, good morning to you, too, little sister. My week is off to a fabulous start. How is yours?"

Kate laughed. "I'm sorry. How are you? I mean it's good to hear that you're doing well. It was great to see you both this weekend. I'm sorry to dispense with the formalities, but my week is off to a rather mysterious start thanks to this donation of unknown origin. Perchance did it come from you and Pepper?"

Rob was quiet for a moment, and Kate heard background noises that suggested that he might be out on one of the oil rigs today.

"Should I call you back?" she asked.

"No, I was just texting Pepper to see if she'd been up to something today. I didn't send the money. I wondered if she did, though I can't imagine that she would without telling me about it."

That did seem unlikely.

"What makes you think it was us? It could've been anyone, couldn't it? You've done a great job getting the word out about the foundation. Maybe someone needed a tax write-off."

"Well, that's just it. If they wanted a write-off, they would've needed some sort of documentation that they'd made the donation. This is a cashier's check made out to the foundation with no name or return address on it."

She stopped short of telling him about the anonymous note that had accompanied it. *Because you and Dr. Thayer make the perfect couple, this check is to cover the amount of your bidding fees. Congratulations and enjoy your date.* It was a little too embarrassing.

"Wait just a minute. Pepper texted me back."

A moment later he said, "Nope, sorry, it wasn't us.

But if you need more money, don't be afraid to let us know."

"Thanks, Rob. I really appreciate the offer. You're a great brother. We're still working on the final total of what we raised Saturday night, but preliminary tallies indicate that the grand total could be edging toward the needed one hundred thousand dollars."

"That's fabulous," he said. "You're doing a great job heading up the foundation. I knew you would, and I'm proud of you."

Rob, who had founded the Macintyre Family Foundation and had served as its chairman of the board, had promoted Kate from director to foundation president about a year ago. Her brother had had a lot of faith in her when he had convinced the board that she was the right person for the job.

She was bound and determined to not disappoint him, and to prove to the board that she was promoted because of her abilities and not just because of her blood tie to the founder of the organization. That was why she'd been working so hard over the past year—and it was one of the reasons she'd had so very little time to date and was so woefully out of practice.

"Thanks, Rob. I appreciate your confidence in me. I know you're busy. So I'll let you go. I have another lead to follow up on with this mystery donation."

"Good luck," he said. "Let me know what you find out."

On Monday morning when Liam exited the elevator to start his hospital rounds, the staff at the nurses' station broke into a round of applause.

He was surprised when he saw Quinn Vogler leading the jubilant reception.

"Well, if it isn't the Ten-Thousand-Dollar Man," said Vogler, who offered a handshake and a good-natured slap on the back. "Well done, my man. Well done."

"Why do you all act like this is such a big surprise?" asked Anna Adams, a registered nurse who worked in pediatrics. "Of course Dr. Thayer would be the one to bring in the most money for the new surgical wing. He's the head of this department."

Liam stiffened, waiting for Quinn to bust him and regale everyone with the story of how Liam had balked at the auction idea in the staff meeting.

But Quinn didn't bite. Instead, he asked, "How long have you and Kate Macintyre been seeing each other? I think that's the biggest surprise of all. She obviously thought you were worth the money."

All gazes were focused on Liam.

"I don't kiss and tell, and I think we all need to get back to work."

"But you're admitting there has been a kiss?" Anna asked.

"For ten thousand dollars, I should hope so," said a female orderly. Everyone laughed. Someone whistled a catcall.

"Where are you taking her on this date?" Vogler asked.

"That's classified information," Liam said.

Vogler narrowed his eyes. "Everything surrounding your participation in the auction and going on the date has been so clandestine. You weren't listed in the program. So we all thought you'd managed to beg off. Now the date's a big secret. What gives with all the mystery?"

Liam frowned and shook his head. He should've been prepared for a grilling. "And as I said before, don't you have patients to see, Dr. Vogler?" Liam quipped. "Way to set the example for the rest of the staff."

At least Quinn had the decency to laugh good-naturedly and make his way toward the general hallway that hosted the patients' rooms. Seizing the opportunity to get away, Liam grabbed his clipboard and did the same.

The first patient on his morning rounds was Billy Barret, a five-year-old boy who had been admitted on Friday with dehydration and flu symptoms. Liam was hopeful that he'd be able to discharge the boy today after evaluating him one more time to ensure that the little guy was still doing as well as he had been yesterday when Liam had popped into the hospital to check on him.

Liam gave three quick raps on the door before pushing it open and stepping inside.

Billy was sitting up in his bed with his legs bent and his feet tucked under them, coloring in a coloring book, making vigorous, broad sweeps with a fat blue crayon. His mother, a single parent, was sitting in a chair across from the boy's bed, looking exhausted, but more relaxed than she had been when he'd spoken to her yesterday afternoon.

"Good morning." Liam nodded to the mother, then crouched down beside the bed so that he was eye to eye with the boy. "How are you feeling today, buddy?"

"Great!" Billy said with all the enthusiasm a five-year-old should possess. He bounced on his knees on the bed. "Can I go home now? *Pleeease?*"

"That's what I'm hoping," Liam said as he flipped open the boy's hospital chart. "I just need to check out a couple things to make sure you're as strong as I think you are."

"I'm strong." Billy flexed his biceps. "Feel my muscles, Dr. Thayer."

Liam reached out and did exactly that. "Yes, sir. I think you've gotten even stronger than you were when you arrived. It must have been all the good food that's made you grow."

Billy scrunched up his face. "*Eww!* No! I don't like the food here. That's why I want to go home. I want to go home. I want to go home. I want to go home." The boy chanted the words and pounded his fists on the mattress.

"Billy, settle down," his mother insisted. The woman had gotten up from her chair and was standing beside the bed with her hands on her hips. "Be still so Dr. Thayer can do his job."

The boy's eyes widened, then he stuck out a quivering bottom lip. His face transformed into a dark cloud that was ready to burst.

"Hey, Billy is my man," said Liam. "I know he's going to cooperate. Aren't you, buddy?"

Caught somewhere between a pout and the verge of tears, the little boy looked back and forth between his mother and Liam. Then he finally nodded and said, "I'll cooperate. I promise."

Liam held up his hand. The boy hesitated for a moment, but then high-fived it.

"I never had any doubt." Liam smiled at Billy and then at the mom. He wanted to tell her he understood how difficult it could be raising a child solo. Working hard to put dinner on the table; worrying about who would watch the kids while the parent was earning a living; dealing with a sick kid without a support system.

"Billy, do you have any brothers or sisters?" Liam asked as he checked the child's eyes with a penlight.

"I have a baby sister," said the boy.

"She's at home," the mother volunteered. Her voice sounded a little shaky. "My neighbor has been watching her."

"Did she manage to escape this flu?" Liam asked.

"So far, I think she has," the mother confirmed.

"That's good." Liam checked Billy's ears. "How about you? Are you feeling okay?"

The mother blinked as if she wasn't sure what to say. But then she let out a breath and seemed to deflate a little. She shrugged. "I feel lousy."

"How long have you had the symptoms?"

"I started feeling bad last night, but it might just be that I'm tired."

"Let me finish with Billy, and I'll take your temperature."

"Thank you, but that's not necessary."

Liam slid the earpieces of his stethoscope onto his ears, but before listening to Billy's breathing, he said, "If you're coming down with this virus, I can give you some antiviral medication that will significantly lessen the severity of your illness."

"But, Doctor, I don't have the money to pay for a prescription like that. My insurance is just a bare-bones plan. It doesn't cover medicines like that. I'm sure it has to be expensive."

Liam shook his head. "Don't worry about it. I'll get you a free sample packet. You need to take care of yourself so that you can keep your kids healthy. We have resources here at the hospital that can help you when you need it."

Liam looked away and put the stethoscope to Billy's back. "Take in a slow deep breath for me, kiddo."

The boy did, and his lungs sounded clear as a bell.

"The good news is you are ready to go home, but I need you to help me with something." Liam was squatting next to the boy again, looking into his eyes. The boy's face turned serious, and he was already nodding, even before Liam could tell him how he needed his help.

"Pal, it looks like your mommy isn't feeling well. She might be coming down with something similar to what you had, and you remember how bad you felt, right?"

The boy furrowed his brow and slid down off the bed to go to his mom. "Are you sick, Mommy?"

"I'm going to be okay, sweetie. Don't you worry."

"But you worried about me," Billy said. "Why can't I worry about you?"

Smart kid, Liam thought as he crossed the room with an ear thermometer in hand. He inserted it in the woman's ear and took her temperature.

"I need you to be in charge of making sure both you and your mommy drink plenty of water over the next few days. What do you say? Will you help me with that?"

Nodding, the little boy stood up a little straighter.

The thermometer beeped, and he checked the reading. Sure enough, she had a fever of nearly 102 degrees.

"I'm going to give you a packet of the antiviral medication, and I want you to start taking it before you and Billy leave to go home. Please get plenty of rest. You might want to see if your daughter can stay at the neighbor's house until your fever is gone. Your son had already promised to make sure both of you stay hydrated. We don't want you to end up here in the hospital."

The woman sighed audibly as if the weight of everything had been lifted off her. "Thank you, Dr. Thayer. We are so blessed to have you looking after us."

"If you get to the point where you feel like you need

help with the kids, please call this number." Liam wrote the help-line direct dial number on the bottom of the discharge papers.

"I completely understand how vulnerable raising children alone renders a parent. Please don't be afraid to reach out for help."

Kate hadn't meant to eavesdrop. Although she had been looking for Liam.

When she'd arrived at the hospital, she'd stopped by the nurses' station looking for him, eager to get confirmation that he was indeed the one who had sent in the ten-thousand-dollar check. The nurse in charge had told her that Dr. Thayer was doing his rounds, and Kate had hoped to catch him as he exited one of the patients' rooms.

She'd been walking by and paused outside of room 307 after she'd heard Liam's voice. The door had been open just enough for her to see inside and witness how wonderfully tender he was to the little boy and his mother. It was a side of Liam she'd never witnessed before, and it formed a snapshot frozen in her mind's eye of him completely in control, but completely without ego.

She knew she shouldn't have lingered and listened, but she couldn't help herself. So many doctors wouldn't have noticed the mother's condition. They might have written it off to worry or exhaustion. So often in their busy workday, when doctors were behind schedule and trying to move as many patients through the hospital as they could—all in the name of improving the bottom line—they didn't have time to notice the subtleties: a sick mother who wasn't well enough to care for a recovering child, and a child who might very well relapse if not given the proper care. But not Liam.

"I'll send in a nurse with the discharge instructions and that medication."

Seeing a softer side of this unpredictable man stirred a wave of tenderness inside Kate that crashed over her before she could realize that the conversation in the room had stopped and that Liam was walking toward the door.

He said goodbye to the mother and son, and Kate barely had time to step back so that it appeared she was just approaching the door as he exited.

"Kate?" he said, looking just as surprised to see her as she was to be face-to-face with him after watching him with his patient and nearly being discovered. The ensuing adrenaline rush made it difficult for her to breathe.

She forced out a greeting. "Hi! Good morning, Liam. Just the man I was looking for." The words tumbled out, and she stumbled over them in the process.

But one look at Liam's smile and she was breathing easier. He seemed genuinely glad to see her.

"Good morning," he said. "To what do I owe this nice surprise?"

"Is this a good time?" she asked. "I know you're doing rounds right now. I can come back later if it would work better?"

"No, this is the perfect time," he said. "I just need to ask the nurse to give this family some meds before they leave. Walk with me, and then we can go get some coffee."

It only took him a moment to relay the request to the nurse who would deliver the patient's discharge orders, and then they made their way to the hospital cafeteria.

He was in such a good mood that it seemed like almost a given that he was the one who sent the check. In fact she held off asking him, believing he might bring it up himself. But by the time the elevator had carried them to the first floor, they had seated themselves in the cafeteria at a table with their coffee, he had talked about his daughters and the weather and the postauction reception his coworkers had given him this morning—calling him the Ten-Thousand-Dollar Man—he still hadn't mentioned sending a check to the office that morning.

"So what brings you to the hospital today?" he asked. "Are you following up on the auction?"

Kate sipped her coffee. "You might say that. I'm following up in a very specific way. This morning I received a large donation for the hospital project. You wouldn't happen to know anything about that, would you?"

"Should I?"

"I've been thinking you might. That's why I'm here. Listen, Liam. I told you I'd pay my half. You only need to contribute the amount you pledged. It was my fault that the bid went up so high. I got carried away."

"You did, didn't you?" There was something in the way he was looking at her, smiling at her—a knowing smile—that nearly made her come undone. "So, what was it that sparked that competitive edge? Why didn't you let Kimela cast the winning bid?"

"I guess that doesn't really matter now, does it?" she said. "What's done is done. The reason I came to see you this morning is to give you back your check."

She pulled an envelope out of her bag and put it on the table between them, pushing it toward Liam.

"What is this?" he asked.

"The ten-thousand-dollar check."

"Why are you giving it to me?"

"I'm giving it back to you. You already gave me a check for your portion of the bid. I'm picking up the other five thousand."

His brows knit as he picked up the envelope and opened it, pulling out the check. After a moment, he returned the check to its envelope and pushed it back across the table toward her.

"This isn't mine. I didn't send this check."

She stared at the white envelope for a confused moment, then looked back at Liam. "If you didn't, who did?"

"And how would I know the answer to that if you don't?" he asked. "Was there a note with it?"

"There was, but it wasn't signed. It only stated that the funds were to cover the bid for our date."

Actually, it read, *Because you and Dr. Thayer make the perfect couple, this check is to cover the amount of your bidding fees. Congratulations and enjoy your date.*

Liam wouldn't write an anonymous note in the third-person, past-tense point of view. What had once made so much sense that it had motivated her to come all the way over here, now made her feel foolish.

"This is crazy," she said. "If not you, who would have the kind of money to do something like this? You don't suppose it was your friend, Kimela, do you?"

Liam laughed. Really it was more of a humorless snort. "Are you kidding? If she did, it would be completely out of character."

They sat in silence for a moment.

"Since our *date* is paid in full, I guess I'll write you a check to refund your five thousand dollars."

Liam shook his head. "You don't have to do that. That check is part of my planned charitable giving."

"So, all along you *planned* to buy your freedom from this auction?" She was being facetious, but he obviously didn't get the joke.

"I hadn't exactly planned for the money to go toward the auction, since I only found out about it a little over a week ago. But I rearranged some things to benefit the auction."

"You mean to buy your freedom?"

He sipped his coffee, his gaze on her the entire time. "I made the donation to ensure a date with you."

She wondered if she'd heard him right. There was a lot of background noise in the cafeteria. It wasn't exactly loud, but the chatter combined with the rattle of dishes and utensils in use, plus the sound of probably big industrial-sized dishwashers being loaded or unloaded had mixed with his words. She wondered if perhaps she'd misheard him.

Rather than ask him to repeat himself, she simply laughed it off. "You do know the main problem with this, right?"

"Problem?" he asked.

"Yes, there's a huge problem."

He looked truly perplexed. "What kind of problem?"

"If we accept your check and the one from the anonymous donor, you won't be able to call yourself the Ten-Thousand-Dollar Man anymore. Think of how disappointed all your coworkers will be. Although I suppose we could alert them that you're changing your name to the Fifteen-Thousand-Dollar Man?"

"My worth keeps going up. I think I like this." He said the words without moving his gaze from hers. "As I said, I'd already moved things around so that I could

donate that money to the pediatric wing. So, my donation will have to stand over and above whatever this
anonymous donor provided. I don't want any hint of
credit for the extra ten grand. Even as much as I love
the thought of the more expensive new name. In reality the hospital will benefit all the more because of it."

"That's so nice of you, Liam," she said. "It really is.
That should be reason enough that you should not feel
obligated to go through with the date."

"Are you telling me you don't want to go out with
me?"

Nerves were pulling at her insides again. "Well, no.
Not exactly. I'm saying I don't want you to feel obligated. I heard you when you said you'd taken yourself
off the market until after your girls go to college. I don't
want you to do anything you're not comfortable with."

"I guess the truth is I wouldn't be entirely happy if
I didn't get to see you again. So, Kate Macintyre, will
you do me the honor of letting me take you out this
weekend?"

There. He'd said it. And this time she'd heard him
loud and clear. The words seemed to flow pretty naturally. She had no idea where this thing between them
was going, but she did know that she'd regret it if she
didn't at least give it a try.

Chapter Eleven

Liam went to great lengths to keep the infamous ten-thousand-dollar date a secret from everyone…including Kate.

He wanted the two of them to have privacy without the media, members of which had been phoning just about every three days to see if he was ready to release the details of his evening with Kate. He also wanted Kate to be surprised.

He'd made a mental note of what she'd mentioned would be her dream date: something low-key and casual, rather than the stereotypical night of limousines and stuffy, expensive dinners.

He'd also done some research to get to know Kate a little better. What had impressed him was that they had a lot of things in common that he hadn't even realized. An interview with Kate in the *Dallas Journal of Business and Development,* published a couple years ago, told her story. Even though she was a high-powered business executive now, she and her oil-tycoon brother had grown up in abject poverty.

Liam had, too. Scholarships, student loans and a little help here and there from Joy's parents had financed his medical school, and had helped them along until he'd been able to graduate and get settled. But even though Liam was educated and financially comfortable now, he'd known his share of hardship growing up.

Much in the same way that Kate had.

The combination of Kate's version of a dream date and the research into their common backgrounds had played into the plans he made.

On Saturday afternoon he picked her up in the Mustang and put the car's top down to begin their *R & R adventure*.

"R & R?" Kate had asked when he had revealed the first part of his plan, which was a drive to a stable to saddle up for a horseback ride.

"Rest and relaxation," he said. "I distinctly remember you telling me your dream date would be shared R & R rather than a hectic fancy affair."

"You're good," she said. "I think we both had our fill of fancy affairs at the auction. I'm glad we're switching gears today."

He slanted her a sidelong glance as the car zipped down the highway. "But never fear. I have plenty of surprises in store for you."

He sensed her sigh more so than heard it above the wind. "For the record, you really didn't have to go to all this trouble."

He shot her another look, a *look* meant to imply that he would rather she not keep saying that. "For the record, I'm happy to be with you today."

She bit her bottom lip. "I am happy to be with you, too."

Their gazes locked, and impulse had him reaching out and taking her hand in his. Something in the air shifted as they rode along, hand in hand, with the sun on their faces and the wind in their hair.

Liam hadn't realized that Kate was such an accomplished rider. His daughter Amanda had suggested Liam take Kate horseback riding as part of the date. If it had been up to Amanda, the entire date would've been centered around horses. The girl was crazy about animals. At least in theory. The girls' mad extracurricular schedule, which had them at the dance studio every night of the week and most weekends, left little time for much else.

Sometimes Liam thought that training this hard at such a young age was a little over-the-top, but the preprofessional dance program the twins were in left no choice. Young dancers were not allowed to choose classes on an à la carte basis. It was a prepackaged program. Enrollees took what they told them to, when they told them to or they took nothing at all. Basically, it came down to the fact that the girls were happy.

And Joy had said it was the best program in the Dallas-metro area. This dance program felt like Liam's last living tie to his late wife.

Glancing over at Kate, who was riding beside him, Liam fought a pang of guilt for allowing Joy to come along on the date.

Kate smiled at him.

He loved his late wife. Always had, always would.

But maybe it was time to allow himself to start living again.

As he adjusted his grip on the reins, the late afternoon sun glinted off his wedding ring, as if Joy were seconding his thoughts and reminding him that the first step toward his future would be to remove his wedding ring.

If this were truly a *real* date, that's what he'd do.

He let Kate get half a length ahead of him, wrapped the reins around his right hand and worked the ring off. He held it between the thumb and index finger of his right hand and looked at it for moment, saying a silent prayer of thanks to Joy for all the good years and for loving him so much that she would want him to move on. She did want that. He was sure he could feel it.

The sun glinted off of it again, as if giving him the affirmative. With that he slid the ring into the small pocket of his jeans, making a mental note to relocate it to a safe place once they got to the end of their ride. He'd arranged for someone to deliver the car to the picnic cabana and take the horses back to the stables. So he'd be able to put the ring in the car's console.

"Everything okay?" Kate asked over her shoulder.

"Everything is great."

And it will just keep getting better.

The next surprise Liam had planned looked like a mirage off in the distance, Kate thought, as they prodded the horses toward two white tents set up on the grassy stretch of private property that belonged to a friend of Liam's. That's all he would tell her—that they would be riding to a *surprise* that was waiting for them, and it was on some property owned by a friend.

"What is this?" Kate asked Liam, stopping her horse in front of two people—a man and a woman—who had come out to greet them and take the horses.

He pointed to the smaller of the two tents. "That's the tent where we will get our massages."

After they handed off the horses, they entered the smaller of the two tents. They were each shown to separate dressing screens, where they slipped out of their clothes and into lightweight robes. As Kate stood behind the screen, naked except for the dressing gown, it crossed her mind that this *could* be awkward, but it wasn't. She was a spa veteran, but this was her first couples' massage.

She found the anticipation quite sensual. It turned out to be very relaxing, soothing her tense muscles and calming any lingering jitters she had about this...*date*.

Tranquil music drifted from hidden speakers as expert hands worked all the stress and kinks out of her body. For a heavenly while, Kate was transported to another plane.

Sometime during the session, Liam must have gotten up and left because when Kate finally lifted her head, he wasn't in the tent.

"Dr. Thayer wanted you to have some time to relax before dinner," said the female therapist.

Kate glanced around the tent and saw that someone had pulled back a curtain and revealed a portable bathtub.

"If I relax any more you'll have to carry me," she said.

The therapist smiled. "Do you need me to help you to the tub?"

Drawing the sheet around her, Kate carefully placed both of her feet on the tent floor. "No, I'm fine. Thank you. In fact, a bath sounds perfect."

"After you finish, please ring the bell." She pointed

to a bell on a silver tray next to the tub. "And someone will be here to assist you with your hair and makeup."

This was definitely shaping up to be a *ten-thousand-dollar date.*

The bath was indeed perfect, its warm water and floral-citrus bath salts washing away any residue of stress. After her hair and makeup were done, she went back behind the dressing screen, hating the thought of putting on the clothes she'd worn earlier. To her surprise, there was a strappy black maxidress, sandals and appropriate new undergarments waiting for her in place of the clothes she had been wearing.

Next to the folded dress was a small box tied with a red ribbon. As she plucked it off the table, her heart kicked into high gear. Had he given her jewelry?

She opened the box and discovered a pair of delicate gold dangly earrings. She gasped. If she had picked out something for herself, it would have been these earrings.

Gently she took them out of the box one by one and put them on. They were the type of earrings that hooked into the ear piercing and didn't have a back, so she gently pinched the wires to ensure they wouldn't fall out of her ears. She studied her image in the small mirror on the dressing table, loving the way the gold glistened against her skin.

For a date that wasn't supposed to be a date, this was shaping up to be a rather sexy evening.

And she loved every moment of it.

After she dressed herself, the woman who had done Kate's makeup led her to the larger tent that was set up next door.

"Dr. Thayer will meet you here for dinner," said the woman. "In the meantime, please relax."

The "dining room" was a medium-sized white tent like Kate had used on more than one occasion to hold special outdoor events. Only this tent was decorated on the inside like none that she had ever seen before. Yards of jewel-toned fabric were swagged from the center of the ceiling outward and draped down the walls; a carpet that looked like a Persian rug covered the floor; a plush sectional sofa lined the walls; and dozens of pillows spilled from the couches onto the floor. In the very center stood a low mosaic table set for a formal dinner. As if that weren't impressive enough, all around her were hundreds of lit votive candles and sprays of flowers.

The scene was an exotic oasis of relaxing coziness made even better with the most delightful aromas wafting in from…somewhere. It didn't matter because Kate had already decided she could happily live here for the rest of her life.

A server had just delivered a glass of champagne on a silver tray when the fabric covering the entrance parted and Liam entered.

He was dressed upscale casual, in a pair of black slacks and a blue button-down. When his gaze met hers, her heart turned over.

"You look gorgeous," he said, crossing the room and giving her a kiss on the cheek.

"You clean up pretty well yourself," she said.

The server offered him a champagne flute and then disappeared.

"Your sister-in-law's catering company made us the picnic supper we're going to enjoy tonight."

"*Picnic supper,* huh? Somehow, I don't think we're going to be eating cold fried chicken and potato salad.

Although, if we did, I'm sure it would be the best cold fried chicken we'd ever tasted."

"Yes, I imagine it would be." He leaned in and touched his glass to hers.

They dined by candlelight—a sumptuous feast of surf and turf, parslied potatoes and green beans almondine. Simple fare prepared to perfection. When finished, the scant waitstaff, provided by Celebrations, Inc., whisked away their dinner dishes and left them with a basket of sweets and chilled bottles of champagne for dessert.

At last they were alone.

"This has been such a lovely evening, Liam. Thank you."

"It's not over yet," he said. "Unless you're ready to call it a night? We haven't had dessert yet."

Strains of a slow bluesy ballad drifted from hidden speakers, and Liam warred with the sudden urge to take her in his arms. It wouldn't be a late evening. Rosie was picking up the girls from a dance rehearsal at nine-thirty and had offered to stay with them until Liam returned. He didn't want to take advantage of her good nature, but he wasn't quite ready for the evening to end just yet.

"I would love to have dessert," Kate said. "Why don't we see what's in the basket?"

The servers had left the basket on the table in front of them. "Why don't you take a look, and I'll pour us more champagne."

"That sounds like a perfect plan," she said.

As he stood and made his way to the silver standing wine cooler, Kate said, "Liam, what is this?"

He turned to see her holding a small wrapped package.

"As much as I would love to take credit for it, I can't," he said. "I don't know what it is. Open it and see."

"Well, I'm glad it's not from you," she said. "You've done too much already. There's a card here with my name on it—let's see what it says."

She chuckled as she read the note to herself.

"What's so funny?" he asked.

"It's from my sister-in-law, Pepper. She says this is a traditional gift that she and her friends Sydney, Caroline and A.J. have given each other for..." She had torn open the paper at one end of the small package. "Oh, no," she said.

He seated himself beside her again, and she turned the package so he couldn't see it.

"What is it?" he asked as he refilled her glass.

Even in the dim light, he could see that her cheeks were flushed pink. She picked up her glass and sipped it.

"I'm definitely going to need more of *this*," she held up her champagne, "before I show you *this*." She gestured to the still-wrapped box.

She took another healthy sip of champagne, looked him square in the eyes and raised her chin a notch. "Condoms. My sister-in-law sent along a box of condoms."

Liam couldn't deny the spark of longing that surged through him. Reflexively his left thumb touched his ring finger, but the band wasn't there.

"I must say, your friends do think of everything."

They both laughed and the sound of their blended merriment melted away the awkward tension.

They unpacked the basket, and he fed her dark-chocolate-covered strawberries, and they shared a piece of what another card described as a flourless chocolate torte. They were so full that they could each only eat a couple of bites.

Maybe it was the champagne that provided the liquid courage or maybe it was that Kate was the first woman in a very long time who was not only able to thaw his frozen heart but warm it to the idea of something more than friendship.

His eyes fell to the creamy expanse of her neck, which looked elegant and smooth in contrast with the black of her dress. He forced his gaze back up to her meet hers.

"Dance with me," he said, standing and pulling her to her feet. She melted into his arms and they swayed to an updated version of "Since I Fell For You."

The feel of her in his arms—the way she fit so perfectly—reminded him of the day they'd first kissed in her office. They had never spoken of that kiss. Still this wasn't how *friends* danced. And that was fine with him. Judging from the way she was holding on to him and swaying with him, she didn't want to put them in the friend zone, either.

It had been a very long time since he'd reveled in the pleasure of soft feminine warmth. Her body, so close and supple, made him yearn to explore the swells and valleys of her shape.

He bent his head, and as if she sensed the subtle movement, she tilted her head up and met his lips. He kissed her gently at first, then more insistently as he drew her closer.

"You are so beautiful," he said, trailing a finger down her jawline. Then his lips followed the path his finger had traced.

Finding her lips again, he pulled her closer. His hands swept over her back, over the place where bare skin met the silky fabric of her dress. They deepened the kiss; her tongue swirling around his in such an inviting and erotic way that he didn't even realize the rasping moan he heard had escaped from his own throat.

His mouth tore away from hers and he pulled back and looked at her, trying to read her, wanting to make sure she wanted what they were dancing dangerously close to. If they were going to stop, they needed to stop now. They needed to say good-night and walk away.

"Are you okay?" he asked.

"I'm more than okay," she said. "And I have a feeling I'm going to be even better before the end of the night."

That was enough to ignite the flame that had been sparking inside him, burning away the last shreds of doubt. All he knew was that he wanted to show her how hot his flame burned for her.

Once again he took possession of her mouth, craving the searing heat of her fingers on his face, in his hair, on his shoulders, trailing down his back, holding him so close he could barely inhale. But her kisses breathed life into him. The feel of her in his arms infused him with hope, happiness and pleasure, emotions he hadn't felt in a very long time.

He couldn't get enough of her, but he had no words to tell her how he felt. All he could do was show her. As he reclaimed her mouth with his more urgently this time, she whispered his name against his lips. With those words, it was as if she'd filled him with hope. For the first time in ages, the heaviness he had been carrying for far too many years was lifted off his shoulders and out of his heart. With her in his arms, he could conquer the world. He held her close and fast, afraid that if he turned loose, she might slip away. He took possession of her mouth, craving the shared heat, reveling in the feel of her fingers on his cheeks, in his hair, on his shoulders, trailing down his arms.

They made their way over to the ocean of pillows and sank down into them.

Need guided his hands as he explored the swell of her breasts, and skimmed her belly until he found the tail of her dress and slid his hand underneath. When his hands found her breasts, she dragged in a ragged breath. As he moved his thumb over her sensitive nipple, a low moan escaped her lips.

Her skin was hot, her body smooth and firm with a sexy feminine power that had him summoning every ounce of self control to keep from taking her right then and there.

They were going to make love.

When the delicious realization racked Kate's body with shudders, she couldn't wait to see what else his body would do to hers.

For Kate, nothing spoke of her trust in a man more than making love with him. Lying with him bare and vulnerable, allowing him to penetrate her personal barriers, inviting him within her body.

Without a word he got up and closed the drapes at the open end of the tent. She watched him pick up the box of condoms her friends had been so smart to include and lowered himself down on the blanket next to her.

She let him undress, aware that there was no place to hide even in the soft candlelight. It wasn't her nakedness that gave her pause as much as it was her emotions. Because surely he could read the hunger in her eyes as clearly as she could read it in his. But he put her at ease when he began placing gentle, unexpected kisses on her body—on her neck, the ticklish spot behind her ears, trailing his way down until he'd reached the sensitive insides of her thighs.

His tongue found its way to her center, and he worked his magic until she cried out in pleasure that was so intense it radiated off her in waves.

He settled between her legs as she looped her arms around his back and pulled him down on top of her.

His gaze locked on hers, Liam thrust gently to fill her. She raised her hips to take him all the way in. His breath escaped in a rush, and he held stock-still for a moment as if he were afraid to break the fragile moment of their joining. Looking into his eyes, Kate reveled in the sensation, in the wonder of his manhood inside her.

His eyes were the deepest shade of blue she'd ever seen. The candlelight flickering off the tent's white walls picked out golden strands in his brown hair, and she ran her fingers through pieces that had curled defiantly in the heat of their passion. She pushed them off his forehead.

It had been a long time since she'd been intimate with a man, but Liam had been worth the wait.

"You feel even better than I imagined," he whispered, before he lowered his mouth to hers for another kiss.

She pulled him closer, giving herself time to explore the muscled feel of him and taste the deliciousness of his mouth—red wine, strawberries and a hint of honey.

When finally she smiled up at him, he began to move. Slower than she expected, each movement driving her mad, making her crave more. Kate rose to meet him halfway, her arms still tight around his back. As he thrust again, he slipped his hands beneath her bottom and shifted her so that he could go deeper. Her body ignited with a passion, fanning a flame from the inside out.

Soon he began pumping his hips with urgent intent. Kate wrapped her legs around his hips at the liquid warmth gathering and radiating outward. Each stroke, deeper and deeper, nudged her closer to release. Her muscles shook from the sheer want of him as she focused on every sensation of every movement. Liam increased his rhythm, and his breathing was heavy and raspy against her ear. His torso was tight as if with the effort to restrain himself for her sake.

When the wave of pleasure crested, a quiet moan escaped her lips. His mouth found hers again. Her release hovered, suspended for a moment that seemed to stretch on into eternity before breaking over her. Liam's kiss caught her cry of pleasure and seemed to fuel his own.

"God, Kate," he groaned, and she arched her body to meet his final powerful thrust.

His eyes closed and his neck tendons strained as the orgasm shook his body. Kate slid her hands along the rock-hard muscles of his arms to end up with her fingers curled into his hair. He swayed above her for a moment before she pulled him down on top of her, and he collapsed, but not before kissing her again as if drawing a sustaining life's breath from the final moments of their coupling.

She curled into the curve of his body and was amazed by the heat radiating from his skin.

"You are so hot," she said.

He smiled at her. "Hey, you stole my line." His voice was raspy, and he was still breathing hard. His was hair mussed, and he looked sexy and beautiful and satisfied. Especially when he planted a gentle kiss on her lips, then pulled her in closer with a possessive arm so that her head was resting on his chest.

His sweet line brought a smile to her face that she

didn't even try to hide. Instead, she ran her palm over his chest, spreading her fingers through the sprinkling of curly dark hair in the valley between his pecs.

On the physical level their lovemaking had depleted every ounce of her energy; yet their joining and the way he continued to hold her replenished and restored her soul.

"I can hear your heartbeat," she murmured, closing her eyes as a satisfied weariness relaxed every muscle in her body. He responded by pulling her closer, and she buried her nose in his neck, reveling in the smell of him.

The piercing sound of a telephone cut through the air, and she felt Liam tense. Gently he disengaged and propped himself up on one elbow and rifled for his pants. "I'm so sorry, but that's my nanny, Rosalinda's, ring tone. I need to take the call. If it were anyone else, it would've gone straight through to voice mail."

"Of course, please," Kate said. As he answered the phone, she grabbed her dress and covered herself with it, reminding herself that Liam was a good dad. Children should always be able to get in touch with their parents…no matter where they were—

"Is she okay?" Liam said, sitting all the way up. "Okay, I'll meet you at the hospital as fast as I can. Please tell her I'm on my way."

"Liam, what is it? Is everything okay?"

His face looked pale and drawn. "My daughter Calee had an accident tonight during her dance rehearsal. They've taken her to the hospital. I need to get there as soon as possible."

Chapter Twelve

Kate went to the hospital with Liam. She'd planned on taking a cab home while he reunited with his family. However, when they arrived, Liam's housekeeper, Rosalinda, and his daughter Amanda met them at the emergency room door. It soon became clear that Amanda would either have to spend the night at the hospital or go home with Rosalinda, who had to watch her grandson that night while her daughter worked.

Before Kate could think twice about it, she offered to ride to Liam's house with Rosalinda and Amanda, and stay with the girl, whose wide frightened eyes were red and sported dark half-moons of exhaustion. Liam declined her offer at first, but when she and Rosalinda pointed out that it wouldn't serve anyone for Amanda to hang around the emergency room at this hour, and Kate's offer to stay with the girl was the only way that Amanda would be able to go to sleep in her own bed, he reluctantly agreed.

As they started to leave, Liam motioned Kate aside. "Thank you for offering to stay with Amanda. I appreciate it. I should've realized from the start that being in her own home in her own bed was the best thing for her."

"I'm happy to help. Is there anything I need to know or should do for her? Has she eaten?"

Liam raked a hand through his hair, frustration written all over his face. It was strange to see the worried parent of a patient rather than the usually stoic doctor.

"I don't know," he said.

"Don't worry. I'll ask her and Rosalinda. We'll figure it out. Are you going to be okay? Do *you* need anything?"

He shrugged.

She reached out and touched his arm. "We'll be fine. You focus on Calee."

His injured daughter was already getting X-rays. Apparently she had landed wrong after performing some sort of pirouetting leap—or whatever the correct ballet term was. It certainly hadn't turned out well.

As Kate turned to join Rosalinda and Amanda, who were waiting near the emergency room exit, Liam said, "I had a different ending planned for our evening."

Kate's cheeks heated as she remembered how it felt to lie naked in Liam's arms. She redoubled her resolve. She was a grown woman; they were consenting adults. She needn't feel ashamed for partaking in the pleasure of intimacy with this attractive man. However, she couldn't help but wonder if the *different ending* Liam had in mind meant that he hadn't planned on them making love or that he hadn't planned on ending up at the hospital. He surely hadn't planned on the hospital. No good parent would ever want that. So she had to wonder if he was already having regrets. But this wasn't the place to worry about that.

Like Cinderella running out of time, the metaphorical clock was striking midnight on this much-anticipated date. Her coach had become the nanny's car; her dress was… Well, it was still beautiful. But her Prince Charming had other subjects to tend to, and it was time for her to return to her life.

"It was a great night, Liam. Thank you for everything. Now it's time for you to focus on Calee. I'll take care of Amanda."

"Thank you," he said.

For a moment, she thought he might lean in and kiss her, but then his gaze zagged off to an unknown spot over her shoulder. Kate turned and saw Amanda standing there watching the two of them with a deadpan expression.

"Get back to your daughter," Kate said, and she turned and walked away.

During the ride to Liam's house, Amanda was silent, but Rosalinda had an idea.

"I will call my daughter and see if she objects to me bringing the baby over to Dr. Thayer's home. He is an infant. He can sleep anywhere. However, it would probably be best if I dropped the two of you off first. I will need to get his things together and load his portable crib into the car. If you don't mind," she spoke to Kate, "you could be there while Amanda takes her shower and prepare her a snack. She is always ravenous after a long rehearsal."

Kate agreed to help in any way Rosalinda needed her.

"Ai, but how will you get home?" Rosalinda asked.

"You do not have your car. I suppose we could load up the children again, but…"

"No worries," Kate said. "I'll call my brother and sister-in-law. One of them will be able to pick me up."

Rosalinda made her call when she got to the house—a stately two-story white Colonial-style home with black shutters and a glossy red front door. Rosalinda's daughter agreed to her mother's suggestion. After Rosalinda showed Kate to the kitchen, the older woman rushed off to gather her grandson.

Alone in the kitchen with the family's mutt dog, Frank, Kate heard water running in another area of the house. She realized Amanda, who hadn't uttered a word since she'd said goodbye to her father at the hospital, must be in the shower. Kate looked around the expansive kitchen at the granite countertops and island in the center of the room, the expensive cherry-stained cabinets, the bulky commercial-grade appliances. Even though Kate wasn't much of a cook—who could justify shopping and cooking for one?—she did feel a pang of envy at the six-burner gas range set under the polished copper vent hood. It was a thing of beauty. It shouted home and family—nourishment for the soul…the way to a man's heart….

She ran her hand over the range's shiny surface as she made her way to the refrigerator to make Amanda a plate of turkey, cheese and fruit. It was simple enough. A snack that she certainly could manage to prepare.

The contents of the refrigerator were so neat and orderly that the fridge looked like it could've been featured in an appliance ad. That was a testament to Rosalinda's handiwork.

Still, the kitchen felt as if it were haunted by Joy. Not *haunted* in a creepy scare-you-off way, but in a sense that this room had the feel of being the heart and soul of the house. Joy had probably designed the kitchen, cooked here, communed with her family here, laughed here. She was very much still here—her essence was part of the walls and woodwork.

As it should be.

After Kate set out all the ingredients for Amanda's snack, she went in search of a plate and silverware, opening cabinets and drawers. She had to admit that she was as intent on discovering clues about the woman who had possessed Liam's heart and soul as she was in finding the dinnerware. But with the exception of a picture of Joy, her hair a riot of strawberry-blond spiral curls, her arms hugging her twin daughters, everything was pretty much standard-issue for an upscale kitchen.

Kate studied the picture until there was nothing more to glean from it. She made a mental note that Liam was not in the photo with *his girls;* she bet that's what he'd called them—all three of them—*his girls.* But really, what more was there to discover here?

Joy hadn't shopped for the food in the pantry; she'd probably chosen the dishes and pots and pans; she may or may not have picked out the dishcloths and towels. But Kate knew that's not what she was so curiously searching for. The answers to the questions she *really* wanted to know were probably hidden in other parts of the house.

She quickly arranged the meat, cheese, strawberries and grapes—the fruit, Rosalinda said, was already washed—on a white plate, which had a raised white grape motif running around the outer edge. She set it on the table at the other end of the kitchen, near an open doorway that she presumed led to the rest of the house. Before crossing the threshold into what looked like a family room, Kate stood stock-still, listening to make sure she still heard the rush of the water running in unknown parts of the house. Once she did, she stepped out of the kitchen and into the *world of Joy*.

This was more like it. Framed pictures adorned every surface—pictures of the girls, pictures of Liam, pictures of Liam and the girls. The same family portrait that he'd shown her hung in a large frame on the wall opposite of the television set. Quickly Kate looked at each one, hungry to discover something…though she didn't quite know what that something was.

It wasn't in this room, even though Joy had probably chosen the furniture and the accessories, the particular shade of sea-foam-green on the walls and the clean, informal white on the rest of the woodwork. The room had an effortless yet pulled-together comfortable vibe about it. Yes, one could cuddle on the couch or huddle around the large square coffee table for game night. It was definitely a *family* room.

Kate glanced back in the direction of the front door, retracing with her eyes the path that she and Rosalinda had taken when the nanny had let them in. They'd passed a staircase…. Good sense told Kate that she had no business venturing upstairs. Not with Amanda showering on the second floor.

Instead of climbing the stairs, Kate made her way along the hallway off the family room. She flipped on a light and opened a door that concealed a small powder room. The earrings that Liam had given her earlier glistened in the light, and once again she realized how much she liked them. A little wave of happiness fluttered in her belly as she shut the door and made her way farther down the hallway.

The sound of her sandals clicking on the hardwood

floor sounded like Poe's "The Tell-Tale Heart." The way
they echoed made her feel like a snoop, and they were
determined to give her away. She shifted her weight so
that they didn't make as much noise. Not that she was
tiptoeing around. She wasn't trying to be sneaky.

And if she kept telling herself that, she might eventually believe it. She paused to look at the photographs
that were hanging on the wall in the hallway: a series of
eleven-by-seventeen-inch black-and-white portraits of
the girls at various ages, digressing chronologically, as
Kate neared an open door at the end of the hall.

Her heartbeat kicked up another notch, as if it were a
Geiger counter indicating that she might be on to some-
thing—or another version of Poe's story, this one titled
"The Tattle-Tale Heart." She flipped on the room's light.
Bingo.

It was the master bedroom. For some reason she
knew it was exactly what she was looking for. Two
antique-looking marble-topped nightstands flanked a
king-size bed. She couldn't help herself; she sat on the
edge of the bed, wondering which side Liam slept on.

An expensive-looking dresser graced the wall directly across from the bed. There, in a silver frame, was
Joy and Liam's wedding picture.

Kate rose from the bed and crossed the room to ex-
amine the photo. A much younger and more carefree-
looking Liam gazed longingly into his beautiful bride's
eyes. The couple's love was so obvious the photo virtually hummed. Kate studied it, her gaze flicking back
and forth between Liam's image and Joy's. It was the
same old test to which she secretly subjected most happy
couples: who was the one in the couple who loved the
most? Usually it was subtle but detectable in a photo.
One person leaning in while the other pulled back ever

so slightly. Or it might have been one person gazing lovingly, longingly, while the other's expression was slightly more removed. It was usually in the eyes.

Hmm... But in this case, it was difficult to discern. In this photo, they had their heads together, both looking equally ecstatic. Having exhausted all the usual clues, Kate set down the photo. Then she spied a pair of worn ballet pointe shoes, the pink satin frayed at the toes. They were tied together by delicate pink ribbons that were unraveling at the ends and hanging from the mirror above the dresser.

The sight of them, so delicate and personal to Joy, revealed something. The feeling deepened when Kate spied an antique jewelry box. She tipped up the lid and saw an array of earrings, bracelets, a wristwatch. She closed it and saw a half-full bottle of Chanel No. 5 on the dresser top, next to a silver hairbrush and comb.

Despite every fiber of good sense that told her not to touch them, Kate couldn't help herself. She picked up the perfume, took off the lid and inhaled. It was the classic scent of a classic lady. She made a mental note never to wear Chanel around Liam since the smell of it would forever remind him of Joy. Kate replaced the cap and returned the bottle to its shrine.

Next she picked up the brush and examined the long, curly light-colored strands still caught in the bristles as if Joy had just this morning smoothed her hair with it.

Carefully, as so not to disturb any of the wisps, she returned the brush to its place. She rubbed her palms on the skirt of her dress as if trying to wipe away all traces of what she'd just learned.

Liam still loved his wife. He still loved her deeply. Even after two years, he kept the most personal of her possessions out and waiting, as if she were just away and would return any moment to use them.

Whether or not he was the one who had loved more in his marriage, he *still* loved Joy. Always had. Always would.

Kate grew up with the very real-life illustration that the only thing worse than being the one in the relationship who loved the most, was being the one who was *in love* with someone who loved the most.

Liam's biggest complaint about Kimela Herring was that she hadn't "heard" him when he'd told her exactly the same thing he'd told Kate: he wasn't interested in a relationship until after his daughters were grown, until they were off at college and well on their way to a life of their own. And who could say if he would be ready to begin again even then?

He'd made it perfectly clear. Kate would be deluding herself if she thought she could be the one to change his mind. That was probably what Kimela had thought. That she was different. The exception to the Liam Thayer rule.

A rush of loss and disappointment flooded through her as she realized she could fall for this man. She was already in way too deep—like quicksand. Her gaze fell back to the wedding portrait. Looking at Joy's radiant face, Kate wondered if it was a sin to have slept with a man who was so obviously still in love with his late wife. Kate had been so blinded by want and need that she hadn't seen it until now.

Kate heard footsteps above her head. Her heart leaped when she suddenly realized that the water was no longer running. Quickly she turned off the light and left the bedroom. She was still in the hallway, but making her way back to the kitchen—where she should've stayed in the first place—when she ran into Amanda. The girl seemed startled to see her.

"What are you doing?" she asked Kate.

"I was just looking for the bathroom. I set out a plate for you in the kitchen. Would you like me to sit with you while you eat?"

Kate fully expected the girl to politely decline, to say that she would just take her plate into the family room and eat while she surfed through the channels. But, much to Kate's surprise, Amanda said, "Sure, that would be great."

Oh.

Kate followed the girl into the kitchen, noticing that she was tall and a little bigger than most ballerinas. But, Kate reminded herself, you never knew what hidden talents people possessed. For all Kate knew, the girl could be the reincarnation of Isadora Duncan.

Good for Amanda for following her passion.

"I didn't pour you a drink," Kate said. "Would you like something?"

"Yes, please. Water would be fine."

Nice manners.

Kate got down two glasses, which happened to be in the same cabinet with the picture of Joy and the girls taped to the inside of the door. She couldn't bring herself to study it as she had before, as if she were... What? Remorseful for snooping? Embarrassed by having realized that the man she'd slept with a couple hours ago was still in love with the image of the smiling woman who lived inside the cupboard with the drinking glasses?

Nope. Joy didn't live in the cupboard; she lived in Liam's heart. This was her kitchen, her house, her hairbrush with strands of her hair still visible. That was her daughter sitting at the table.

Kate had no right to any of it.

She said a silent apology—unsure if the contrition was for Joy or herself—for all she wanted and would never know, not with this man. She shut the cabinet door. With that gesture, she tried her best to close off all hope of anything more than friendship with Liam Thayer.

But could she really just be friends with Liam after having made love to him, after she had left a little piece of her heart behind that she would never regain?

Unlikely.

She pushed the thoughts out of her head and filled each glass with ice from the freezer door and then water from the adjacent dispenser.

As she carried them back to the table, she racked her brain for conversation starters appropriate for teenage girls.

But Amanda was one step ahead of her.

"Did you wear that dress horseback riding?"

Oh, that's right. This must be the daughter who loves horses. Liam had told Kate that one of his daughters was enamored with them.

"No, I was wearing jeans and boots earlier," Kate said. "I changed for dinner."

She refused to think about how Liam had picked out the dress, about how they had gotten a couples' massage and relaxed to the point of losing good sense and ravaging each other's bodies.

For God's sake, she was with his daughter! She pushed all those thoughts out of her head.

"Do you like to ride?" Kate asked.

The girl perked up more than she had all evening. "I love to. Although I don't get to do it very often."

Before Kate could stop herself, she'd blurted out, "I

live on a ranch. You should come by sometime and take out one of the horses."

"Can I come over tomorrow?"

"Oh, well, I don't know. You'll have to ask your dad."

Maybe she shouldn't have mentioned the ranch. She was only trying to make conversation. There was probably no way Liam would bring the girl out there. It would have to be Liam's decision. Beyond that, it wasn't something for her to choose.

"Did you know you're missing an earring?" Amanda said.

Kate's hands flew up to her ears. Sure enough, the right ear was bare. Her heart started pounding. Both earrings had been in place when she'd peeked into the hall powder room. She'd stopped to admire them in the mirror.

That meant that one of her earrings had fallen off somewhere between the kitchen...and Liam's bedroom.

Kate had no idea how she would retrieve it, much less explain how it got wherever it landed. What in the world had she been thinking when she had so brazenly set off to explore the house that Joy built?

Chapter Thirteen

"Why are you still up?" Liam asked Amanda when he entered the family room and saw her stretched out on the couch in front of the TV.

"I wanted to stay up to make sure Calee is okay," his daughter said. "Where is she?"

Amanda sat up and pushed her mane of blond curls out of her eyes and looked around as if she expected her sister to hobble into the room. Amanda had her mother's curly hair, Liam thought. And her eyes. His left thumb searched his ring finger for the wedding band touchstone, but it wasn't there. It was still in the car's console. He'd forgotten to bring it in, and would have to go out and get it as soon as Amanda went to bed.

"She hit her head when she fell, and they wanted to keep her overnight for observation. She also sustained a pretty bad fracture. They can keep her comfortable with medication tonight. We'll go get her tomorrow."

Amanda hugged a pillow to her chest and looked a little deflated. "I tried to call you, but you didn't answer."

Liam pulled his phone out of his pocket and pressed the button to bring it to life. Sure enough, five missed calls.

"I'm sorry, Amanda. I had to silence the ringer when I was in the emergency room. Is everything all right?"

Amanda shrugged and pouted.

"She is just worried about her sister, Dr. Thayer," said Rosie. "Please do not be mad. I am the one who told her that she could stay up until you got home."

Liam gave a curt nod. He wasn't mad at anyone. It had just been a long day with a lot of things to process. Like Calee's accident.

And his unexpected intimacy with Kate. He really hadn't set out to seduce her. They just seemed to have no control when they were around each other. Right now, he was so exhausted and drained he wasn't sure if their attraction was a good thing or not…. But where was she?

"Is Kate still here?" he asked, fairly certain that she would be sitting here if she were.

"She called someone to pick her up after I got back with Joaquin."

Oh, yeah. Liam dragged a hand over his eyes, then blinked, trying to right his thoughts. He'd been so scattered since learning that Calee was hurt. It was different being at the hospital as the parent of a patient than being the doctor in charge. But, right, Rosie was supposed to watch her grandson tonight while her daughter worked. Yet she was here.

"Where is Joaquin?"

"He is upstairs in the guest room, asleep in his portable crib. Maria allowed me to bring him here tonight, so that I could watch him and be with Amanda. That way Ms. Macintyre was able to go home."

He also hadn't intended for Kate to have to find her own ride home. He'd call her soon and apologize. Again his left thumb explored the bare base of his ring finger. He warred with a sensation that felt a lot like regret. But regret for what? That he'd been human and had spent a lovely evening with a woman he was exceptionally attracted to? He blinked away the question. He'd have to sort that out later.

"I appreciate you being here, Rosie," Liam said. "Sometimes I don't know what we'd do without you."

"Kate has horses, and she invited me to come over and ride tomorrow," Amanda said. "Can I go?"

What? Another odd sensation shot through him; this time the feeling was more akin to irritation. Why was Kate inviting his daughter over? Especially when she knew that his other child was hurt. Maybe she wanted to give Amanda something to do while they got Calee settled.

But he couldn't deny the nagging feeling that reminded him of how Kimela Herring had dangled special ballet workshops that were only available to the most elite and promising dancers in front of his daughters. Soon it had become clear that she was using them to get to him. He gritted his teeth. He'd vowed that would never happen again.

While he couldn't be sure that's what Kate was doing when she'd invited Amanda over, he did know it was going to create conflict with his daughter because he was not going to have time to take her over there. But now wasn't the time to break the news to Amanda. They were both overtired and irritable. The best thing they could do was go to bed.

"Can I go?" Amanda insisted.

"Amanda, you need to go to bed," he said.

"But, *Daad.*" She sat up and slammed down the throw pillow onto the couch cushion.

"'But, Dad' nothing. Go to bed."

"You don't even love me. You don't even care. Everything is for Calee. You wouldn't even take my calls tonight." Amanda got up and stormed out of the room.

"Amanda!" Liam called.

Rosie was already on her feet and headed toward the stairs. "I'll go see about her and calm her down, Dr. Thayer." Rosie paused at the threshold and turned back. "I don't mean to tell you what to do, but I would suggest taking a few minutes for you both to catch your breath, and then coming up and saying good-night. She's just worried about her sister. Please don't go to bed mad."

He nodded. Rosie was right. If he'd learned one thing since losing Joy, it was that life was fleeting and fragile. There were no extra seconds to waste on being mad.

Being irritated with Kate for the presumptuous offer to his daughter was another matter. But there was nothing he could do about it now other than put it out of his mind so that he wasn't still stewing when he went up to say good-night to Amanda.

He retrieved his ring from the car. As he walked down the hall toward his bedroom, force of habit had him sliding the gold band onto his ring finger where it belonged. Only his finger was so swollen, he couldn't get it past his knuckle. A raw and primitive grief overwhelmed him. He couldn't put his wedding ring back on.

Not after tonight.

His body ached, and he needed a shower. He would rinse off quickly, then go up to tuck in his daughter and call it a night. Tomorrow was another day.

He closed his bedroom door, set the ring on the dresser and unbuttoned his shirt before he sat down on the edge of the bed to remove his shoes. When he bent to untie the laces, something shiny lying in the middle of the floor between the bed and the dresser caught his eye. At first glance he thought maybe his ring had rolled off the dresser. He kicked off his shoes and walked over to pick it up.

But it wasn't his ring.... It was an earring. And it looked just like one of the pair he'd given Kate tonight. Liam stiffened. How had it gotten in here? Had Rosie dropped it when she was cleaning? But how would Rosie get it?

He glanced around the room at the pile of dirty clothes that needed washing and another pile that needed to go to the dry cleaner. Obviously Rosie hadn't worked her way into the master bedroom. But *someone* had.

When Liam set the earring on the dresser, he noticed that the pale pink ribbon that usually lay atop Joy's jewelry box was on the dresser, not where it should be. He reached out and rotated the bottle of Chanel No. 5 a quarter turn so that the writing on the bottle faced forward. The way it should've been.

Somebody had definitely been in here, and tomorrow, when he called to politely decline the horseback riding invitation and to ask if someone was missing an earring, he would ask Kate what she'd been doing in his bedroom.

The following Friday, as Kate stood in front of the drugstore prophylactic display, she had the sudden urge to turn up her collar and don her dark glasses. She'd never purchased condoms before. In her limited sexual experience, the man had always taken care of the task and had come prepared.

As she stood there with so many…choices, suddenly her plan to replace the box that Pepper had sent in the dessert picnic basket with an unopened box and give them back to her tonight didn't seem like such an airtight plan.

She had a good memory. So she thought she'd remember what kind of box they'd come in, but… She hadn't realized there would be so many choices and the boxes would all look so similar. Now that she was standing here, nothing looked familiar. Why hadn't she at least taken a picture of the packaging with the camera on her phone?

Instead, she glanced at the clock on her phone. She was due at Pepper and Rob's in twenty minutes, and she still had to stop by her house and pick up a bottle of wine. She'd mistakenly thought that this would be a slightly mortifying but quick trip to the drugstore. All she needed to do was smugly present the unopened box to her sister-in-law, proving that no matter what Maya the Matchmaker had said, there had never been anything between Liam and Kate. Never had, and there certainly never would be now.

Kate flinched as a tall guy with close-cropped dark hair passed by the aisle. It would be just her luck that she'd run into Liam here, now…. But that guy wasn't Liam. And it hadn't been him the other eight times she'd thought she'd seen him over the past five days.

Come on, Kate, get a grip. This isn't the ninth grade. Celebration was a small town. The odds favored her running into Liam sometime. Even though she'd popped into a drugstore outside of Dallas on her way home from work to keep from running into anyone she knew.

Still, she hoped the fateful event would happen later…much later…years later. Or at least after Liam had the opportunity to get over himself. She still stung from the embarrassment of his phone call Sunday night.

It had been bad enough that Amanda had obviously misunderstood Kate when she'd said the girl could come out to the ranch and ride *sometime. Teenagers.* It probably *would* be a good thing for Liam to wait until his daughters were out of the house before he dated. Obviously he was carrying too much baggage to maintain a healthy relationship with a woman who wasn't his late wife.

It's not fair to blame Joy. Kate silently admonished herself. She had been fully cognizant and in charge of herself when she'd gone snooping in his bedroom. She simply hadn't planned on the earring falling out of her ear while she was there. And she hadn't planned on Rosalinda showing up so soon after Amanda had pointed out that the earring was missing.

Gaaah! She should've known better. She *always* got caught when she tried to be sneaky. And since she wasn't able to retrieve the earring, she should've been prepared for Liam's line of questioning.

She shuddered and covered her eyes with her hand as she recalled the awkward silence following his questions, "Are you missing an earring, Kate?" *Silence.* "How did it get in my bedroom?" *Silence.* "Were you looking through things on my dresser?"

All she could manage to say was, "I'm sorry, Liam. I was curious."

Instead, she wished she would've said she would mail the other earring back to him. And then she should have asked him what the heck *he* was doing giving her a sexy black dress and pretty gold jewelry? And making love to her like that?

What was *that?*

If there were a kingdom called *Mixed Signalia,* Liam Thayer would be its king.

No! What she *should've* said was, *maybe Kimela Herring "didn't hear you," but, buddy, I hear you loud and clear. I don't need your baggage. I have enough of my own.* And then she should've told him if he really wanted to do what was best for his daughters, he'd continue with the grief counseling so that he could get to the root of his issues.

Well, no, she wouldn't have brought the girls into it.... But couldn't she have come up with something better than *I'm sorry, Liam. I was curious?*

Ugggh! She pressed her palms to her eyes as if the gesture might blot out the memory.

"You okay?" asked a husky voice from behind her.

Kate flinched and flushed as she realized a stranger was standing behind her, and she had no clue how long he'd been there. She blinked, trying to rid her vision of the white spots she was seeing after pressing on her eyes.

The guy cleared his throat. "Uhm, my wife likes those," he said, hooking his thumb toward a black package with yellow writing, and sounding almost as embarrassed as she felt.

"Thanks." Without looking at him she grabbed the suggested package and beelined for the checkout counter before she humiliated herself any more than she already had.

If she couldn't remember the specific kind of rubbers, chances were that Pepper wouldn't, either. Anyway, she did remember that the box had some yellow on it—or was it orange?

Whatever. This was close enough. She just needed to get out of here.

As luck would have it, there was no line at the register. She paid for her purchase and a candy bar for her little nephew, Cody, tucking both into her purse before she left the store. As she started her car, her cell phone rang. The name Darrell Friday—a nice-looking drug rep she'd met on Monday in a meeting in the hospital's fund-raising department—cropped up. She'd managed to avoid Liam, but she'd run into Darrell twice in the elevator. On their way out to the parking lot, he'd mentioned it might be nice if they met for a glass of wine sometime.

She'd given him her business card because she thought she might want to go—to remind herself that some men were interested in her even if Liam wasn't. Darrell had been calling every evening, but she hadn't called him back. *Not* because she was holding out for Liam, but because she wasn't interested in Darrell. So what was the point?

As with all his other calls, she let this one go to voice mail, too. If the guy persisted into next week, she'd call and let him down easy. She was simply too busy with the final stretch of fund-raising for the pediatric surgical wing.

It was because of *work*.

It certainly had *nothing* to do with Dr. Thayer.

She turned down the long driveway on the property she shared with her brother and Pepper. Kate had a cozy two-bedroom bungalow situated a couple acres behind her brother and Pepper's sprawling home. Kate had just enough time to pop into her house, grab a bottle of wine and get over to Pepper and Rob's.

When she rang the doorbell, her sister-in-law greeted her with a warm hug. The delicious aroma of something that smelled Italian and garlicky wafted out to tease her.

"You're here! You're here!" she said. "I have been waiting all week to hear about the ten-thousand-dollar date. Rob's not home yet. So we can have a little girl time. But he'll be here any minute. So start talking. I am not even going to wait until we have glasses of wine in hand. Was it fabulous?"

Kate had to resist the urge to say, "No, it was a train wreck."

She did an instant *refocus, reframe,* reminding herself that Pepper was like a romance bloodhound. That was commentary on her sister-in-law's looks. With her long blond hair and brown eyes, Pepper was gorgeous. She was also persistent. Once she got the scent of possible love in the air, she was relentless in trying to bring the couple together. Obviously there would be no great romance between Kate and Liam, but Pepper, probably fueled by the notions that Maya had put into her head, was convinced that Liam and Kate were destined to be soul mates. That meant that Kate had to be careful what she said. Apathy was the only thing that would throw Pepper off the scent.

"It was fine," Kate said, doing her best to sound blasé, if not a shade unimpressed. "But it's done and now we resume our regularly scheduled lives."

Pepper stood in the foyer frowning at Kate, clearly disappointed with the lack of fireworks.

"It was fine?" Pepper asked. "*Fine?* That doesn't sound good."

Kate pursed her lips before she spoke. "Honey, you have no idea."

"What?" Pepper asked.

"Nothing." Kate shook her head and gave her sister-in-law the open-palmed shrug.

Pepper's gaze narrowed. "There's something you're not telling me."

"Don't be ridiculous," Kate protested. "If there was something to tell, I'd tell you. He hasn't called for another date. So obviously there's nothing there. In fact, I'd like to return these."

Kate opened her purse and pulled out the brand-new box of condoms, smug and pleased with her cover.

There. That should silence her. That's what Pepper was fishing for. For all intents and purposes, everything was *fine* and nothing had happened.

As Pepper and Rob's son, Cody, appeared in the hallway, Pepper grabbed the box and tucked it under her arm.

"Aunt Kate!" The young boy threw his arms around Kate's middle and nearly hugged the stuffing out of her. "I'm so glad to see you."

"I'm happy to see you, too, sweetie." Kate knelt down in front of the boy so she could be at eye level with him. "How was school?"

She was glad to see Cody so strong. He had been through a series of operations that had helped him regain his ability to walk again after a tragic car accident that had claimed the life of Kate and Rob's father. The crash had nearly cost them Cody, too.

After Kate's miscarriage, she'd consoled herself with the thought that, even if she didn't have a child of her own, she was blessed to have her nephew, Cody, to love. He was enough. He was more than enough, because

Kate definitely subscribed to the theory that the happiest people were satisfied with what they had. They didn't waste time brooding over what eluded them.

She had her little family. So even if she never found a love of her own, she was…happy. And she refused to let the image of Liam or the pang of *what might have been* shake her out of her good mood.

The last thing she needed was to fall in love with a man whose heart would always belong to another woman. Cody was still here. That was a miracle. What right did Kate have to want for anything more?

"Look what I brought you." Kate pulled the candy bar out of her purse. "Give it to your mommy. Don't eat it before dinner, okay?"

Pepper was Cody's stepmother. Rob's first marriage had ended in divorce. Sadly Cody's birth mother wanted nothing to do with the boy, which proved to Kate that some people were just not capable of love. Because how could anyone turn her back on such a precious kid?

Of course the fact that Pepper loved Cody enough to make up for his natural mother's failing proved that some people were capable of boundless love. But Kate knew that Liam wasn't capable of boundless love. His heart belonged to his late wife and his daughters. And that was fine. It was a good thing she'd realized it before she'd slipped any deeper into the quicksand of unrequited love.

"Mommy! Look what Aunt Kate gave me."

"Wow! That looks yummy. Let's put it up here for now, and if you eat a good dinner, you can have some of it for dessert."

Cody happily obliged and then went off into the other room to play a predinner video game.

* * *

"It's an unopened box of twenty-five condoms."

"Right." Kate shifted in her seat, but took care to keep her face neutral.

"The box I gave you was our lucky condoms," Pepper said.

Kate pulled a face. "Okay. I don't understand."

"Clearly," Pepper said. "Let's suffice to say that we could call it the sisterhood of the traveling condoms. It started with A.J. and has been passed on to each of us. Everyone who uses a condom from that box ends up marrying the guy."

Pepper's eyes sparkled.

Kate had no idea that the box had been around. "If there are condoms left over, that must mean there's not much action going on. And that means it's a good thing we retired the box, because if it gets past its prime, it could become the box of unlucky condoms. That would not be an occasion to celebrate."

"So, you're telling me you and Dr. Thayer *didn't*...?"

"I'm telling you that Dr. Thayer has too much baggage."

"Oh!" Pepper's eyes widened. "Speaking of baggage, I found out the dirt on what happened between him and Kimela Herring."

Kate sipped her wine, not wanting to seem overly eager to hear the details. "Really?"

Pepper set down the knife she'd been using to chop hearts of palm for their salad. "Remember how I told you that Kimela pulled some strings to get the girls into a residential slot with the Randolph Ballet in New York City? From what I understand, one of the girls is the better ballerina of the two. Is her name Calee?"

Kate shrugged. "He has a daughter named Calee,

but I've not met her, and I don't know if she's the better dancer."

Kate remembered thinking that Amanda didn't look like a natural-born ballerina, but that didn't mean the girl couldn't dance.

"Anyway, Kimela made sure that both girls were accepted into the program. From what I understand, with the kids essentially off at boarding school, she thought she'd be free to move in with Liam. Can you believe the audacity?"

"Yes, he'd mentioned that Kimela didn't 'hear him,'" Kate said and immediately regretted the slip.

"Really? Do tell."

"Oh, that was basically it. You know, I asked him why Kimela would bid ten thousand dollars on him. He'd said something about her being a friend of Joy's and pushing a little too close for comfort. He claims that he doesn't even want to date until after the girls are in college. That's why we came up with the fake date in the first place."

Pepper was standing there watching Kate intently. She had her head cocked to one side and her hand on her hips. A bloodhound that had picked up a scent. Kate felt as transparent as a picture window. Quickly she replayed the conversation in her head.

To cover she added a brusque, "The guy is just emotionally unavailable."

"Maybe to Kimela Herring," Pepper said. "But she's about as subtle as a rhino charging the Serengeti."

Kate shrugged.

"Give him time," Pepper said. "I saw how he was looking at you after the auction."

"Well, yeah. I'd gone five thousand dollars over his

budget. He was probably looking at me like he wanted to kill me."

"Kill you? No. Ravage you?" Pepper nodded. "Yep. And now you return a brand-new unopened box of condoms. Gosh, if I were Shakespeare, I might say something like *the lady doth protest too much, methinks.*"

Pepper's words hung in the air, and Kate could feel her face growing increasingly hotter.

"Honey, it's okay," Pepper said. "In fact, it's the most wonderful thing to be vulnerable for someone you love."

Chapter Fourteen

On Saturday morning Liam thought he would have to hog-tie Amanda and carry her out to the car. He didn't know what was going on in her head. Since Calee had been injured, Amanda had balked about going to her dance rehearsals. She kept saying she wanted to stay home with Calee.

He wondered if her sister's injury had reopened the emotional trauma she'd experienced when her mother had died in the car accident. He'd tried to talk to her about it, reassuring her that Calee was going to be just fine. But the reasoning didn't seem to help.

This morning she was fighting him tooth and nail.

Normally he would've just let her stay home, but the dance school was nearing the final rehearsals for their end-of-the-year dance showcase. Plus they were already in a bind because Calee, who had been cast to dance several of the lead roles, was out for the rest of the season.

Amanda had supporting roles that were just as important to the production as a whole. Liam was getting tired of telling her over and over that the other dancers were depending on her. If she missed a rehearsal, it would leave a hole in the dance, and it wouldn't be fair to her castmates. She had to go. End of discussion.

Reluctantly she got into the car and sulked the entire way to the studio.

"Look," Liam said as he pulled into a parking place and stopped the car. "You only have a few weeks left. You made a commitment, and you have to see it through. You know that's our house rule."

"Can I quit next year?" she asked.

Her question caught Liam off guard. She loved dance. It was probably just spring fever.

"Is that what you want to do?" he asked. "It's always been such a big part of your life, and you know Calee doesn't want to quit."

It was true. While he'd had to force Amanda to go today, he nearly had to tie Calee down to keep her home. She'd begged him to let her go watch. But she hadn't wanted to go in the wheelchair; she'd asked if she could just go sit in a regular chair. But Liam knew she'd end up hobbling around to go to the bathroom or to talk to friends. If she did that, she might end up injuring herself worse.

Again Liam had to be the bad guy and make her stay home.

Amanda simply shrugged off his question.

"You don't have to decide now. In fact, you have until sign-up in the fall to consider it. Maybe take the summer off and see if you miss it."

"Can I do horseback riding instead?"

So *that* was what this was about? Kate's offer for

her to come out and ride. Irritation roiled in his gut. "I don't know," he said. If he did let her take lessons this summer, it would probably be best to find a place other than Macintyre Ranch.

For some reason the reality of that didn't feel quite right, either.

"We can talk about it later," he said. "You need to get inside so that you're not late."

Amanda grabbed her big dance bag that contained the various shoes and dance gear she needed for the different numbers she was in…and, judging by the size, possibly the kitchen sink and a few farm animals. She shut the door without saying goodbye.

Liam drew in a deep breath and backed out the car. He was really getting fed up with her attitude. But now, before this rehearsal she didn't want to attend anyway, wasn't the time to open that discussion. They'd talk about it tonight. Maybe the horseback riding could be a reward for a much-improved disposition.

Kate's face and how she'd looked that night as they had made love was stuck in his head. He glanced down at his still-bare left ring finger. He hadn't in good conscience been able to put his ring back on since that night.

He sighed. Maybe he was the one who needed time to sort things out. Obviously he was just as confused and out of sorts as his daughter.

On the third Saturday of each month, the Macintyre Ranch opened its stables to special-needs children in the Dallas area. The program called Kids' Day was sponsored by the Macintyre Family Foundation and had been well received by the community as a service to aid in bully prevention and increased understanding of special-needs children. It was a two-pronged program: one branch bringing in the kids with special needs and the other securing children in the community who wanted to help.

The program had been in place for almost a year and had gotten to the point where Kate could rely on her assistants to run it without her. Still, since she lived on the ranch anyway, she liked to drop by for an hour or so and watch the kids interacting.

Animals were a great equalizer, something over which all people—no matter their abilities—could bond. The laughs, smiles and all-around goodness that came from Kids' Day always restored her faith in humanity.

They were hosting an unusually large group today, so Kate and her assistant, Rebecca, had rolled up their sleeves to help. They had just finished giving the kids a hay ride around the property and were going to pet a foal, when Kate thought she saw Liam's daughter Amanda out of the corner of her eye over by the barn door. But when she looked around, the girl wasn't there.

This was getting ridiculous. First she had phantom sightings of Liam. Now she thought she was seeing Amanda?

It had been one week since their date. Tomorrow it would be a week since the phone call in which he had firmly let her know where they stood. Actually where they *didn't* stand; there was nothing between them.

With a heavy heart she reminded herself that she needed to get over it and move on.

She turned her full attention to the kids and helped usher them into the stable where Caleb, one of the ranch hands, was trotting out the chestnut foal.

That's when she saw movement in her peripheral vision again. This time she turned quickly, and there stood Amanda in plain sight. Her posture was slightly hunched. She looked awkward and uncomfortable in her pink Hello Kitty T-shirt. Below her denim shorts, her lanky legs a little knock-kneed, she almost looked a little like a foal herself. Her curly blond hair was pulled back into a tight ballerina bun. She'd moved closer to the group and didn't duck behind the wide post she was standing next to, which is what she must have done before.

Great. What was she doing here? Kate glanced around searching for Liam, but she didn't see him. There was no way he would've dropped off his daughter.

Even so, not wanting to take her frustrations out on the girl, Kate waved. Amanda waved back.

Suddenly Kate sucked in a breath.

Oh, no. Please tell me she didn't...

"The kids are settled," Kate said to Rebecca. "Will you be okay if I leave for a moment? I need to see about something."

"Sure," said Rebecca. "Take your time. I've got you covered."

"Thanks, Becs."

Kate walked over to Amanda. "Hi. I'm surprised to see you today."

The girl flashed a shy, sheepish grin and ducked her head a little. "You said I could come out and ride sometime."

"I did, didn't I?"

Amanda nodded. "Can I? Right now?"

"Well, as you can see, we have a pretty full house."

"Who are those kids?"

She motioned for Amanda to follow her as she told her about the Kids' Day program.

They sat on the porch steps of her brother's office.

Rob was out of town today on business. Kate figured this was probably the best place for Amanda and her to talk.

"That sounds really cool," Amanda said. "Can I help you with the kids and ride after they leave?"

"Amanda, does your dad know you're here?"

The girl nodded her head vigorously. A little too vigorously for someone telling the truth.

"He does, huh? How did you get here?"

The teen ducked her head again, then glanced up at Kate from beneath long, naturally dark lashes she'd obviously inherited from her father. The memory of Liam's blue eyes and how he'd looked at Kate—before last weekend—made her feel as if she were the only person in the world he did see. That revelation struck her forcefully.

"I walked." Amanda's voice was thin.

"All the way from your house?"

The girl didn't answer.

"That's a very long walk. I'm surprised your dad let you walk all that way alone."

Amanda shrugged and looked away.

Kate was horrified by the thought that the girl had walked here. The road between the ranch and Liam's house was mostly a two-lane highway. But then Kate had a thought. It was odd that the girl was wearing a shellacked ballerina bun with her casual clothes.

Something didn't add up.

Kate fished her cell phone out of her pocket. "I think you should call him and let him know you made it safely."

The girl recoiled from the phone that Kate was trying to hand her. "Oh, no, I don't need to do that."

Amanda looked as if, were she to touch it, the thing

would burn her. Kate had an inkling that calling her dad and telling him that Amanda was at the ranch just might do that.

"He doesn't know you're here, does he?"

Amanda stared at her hands for a long while before she finally said, "No," in a tiny voice.

"Are you supposed to be at a dance class?" Kate asked.

Amanda gave a one-shoulder shrug accompanied by "Yeah, I guess."

"Don't you think everyone is going to worry about you when they realize you're missing and they don't know where you've gone?"

"They won't care. They probably won't even see that I'm not there."

Kate set her cell down out of sight from Amanda. "Oh, I think you'll be surprised by how fast they'll find out you're gone and how much they will miss you. Why would you think they wouldn't?"

"I'm not good at dance. Calee is the one who's talented. Everyone is all worried about how they're going to replace Calee in the showcase. But I'm pretty much invisible. But that's okay. I really don't even like dance."

"Why not?" Kate asked.

"Besides the fact that I'm really bad at it," she began, "all the kids are mean. Especially now that Calee isn't there."

"They're mean to you?" Kate asked.

Amanda nodded. "Calee is so good at dance. She's like the queen around there," Amanda said. "She won't let them give me a hard time. It's all because of Mrs. Herring getting me into that Randolph dance program. I didn't even want to go, but Calee did. She got in, but

I didn't, and we knew that our dad wouldn't let her go alone. So Mrs. Herring got me in.

"I guess she paid them or something. Because I'm not good enough to go there, and everyone knows it. When I told my dad I really didn't want to go to New York, when he said we didn't have to—that Calee would have other chances—I was glad. But now at dance everyone is supermean to me. Calee says it's because they're just jealous because I could've gone to New York if I'd wanted to."

"Was Calee mad at you for not wanting to go?"

"No. She never gets mad at anything. Except when someone treats me bad. She's kind of protective of me."

Kate smiled at the girl, sensing that Amanda probably didn't have many people she could talk to about this, if she was spilling her guts so freely right now.

"Well, that's really nice," Kate said. "You're lucky to have such a good relationship with your sister. Don't worry about what the other girls say. If they're mean, they don't matter."

Amanda gave another one-shoulder shrug as if she wasn't fully convinced.

"There was this really smart lady named Eleanor Roosevelt," Kate said. "Have you heard of her?"

"Of course. She was the president's wife."

Smart kid. "She used to say the only way people can make you feel inferior is if you allow them to. Makes sense, doesn't it? If you don't let them make you feel bad, then they lose all their power over you."

Amanda nodded. "It's hard, though."

"I know it is, kiddo."

Kate thought about Liam, about how she'd allowed him to make her feel so foolish for being curious about his life and his marriage to Joy. Going into his bedroom and looking may not have been the best idea, but it certainly wasn't a crime punishable by law. A thought, sudden and sickening, settled around her.

Her snooping wasn't the root of the problem. He'd gotten scared, and it had simply given him a tangible reason to disengage. Yep. The man wasn't ready for another relationship. Kate wouldn't torture herself with waiting around, hoping he would change his mind.

She certainly wasn't going to let him make her feel bad when she called to tell him that his daughter had walked to Macintyre Ranch. Kate wouldn't take it out on this sweet, vulnerable child who had already suffered far too much sorrow for her tender age. But if Liam tried to pull the switcheroo blame game on her again, she wasn't going to have any part of it.

"Have you told your dad you dislike dance as much as you do?"

"Sort of but not really. We kind of talked today about me taking the summer off from dance camps so that I could think about it. But I don't think I can really quit."

Kate frowned. "Now, wait. I thought you told me that you really hated it? Did I hear you wrong?"

"No, I do hate it."

Kate reached out and put a hand on the girl's arm. "Honey, life is too short to torture yourself with something you hate. I hear the program you're in is pretty stringent. Your dad loves you and wants you to be happy. I'm sure if you talked to him and told him everything you told me, he would let you do something else."

"Like horseback riding?"

The suggestion gave Kate pause. She needed to weigh her words carefully so that the girl didn't think Kate was extending an open invitation for Amanda to walk over here anytime she got the whim.

"Or something like that. I'm sure your dad could find a program for you…somewhere. You just need to tell him."

"I can't. And I can't leave dance. No matter how bad I am."

Okay, this conversation was starting to feel like the Abbott and Costello "Who's on First?" routine. The more they talked, the more it confused Kate.

"Will you tell me why you can't leave if it's making you so miserable?"

Like a sudden cloudburst, Amanda started crying.

Kate scooted over and put her arm around Amanda. "Oh, honey. Please don't cry. I'm sorry. You don't have to tell me if you don't want to."

The teen sobbed for a minute, and Kate wished she had a hankie or a tissue she could offer Amanda. But Kate didn't want to abandon the girl while she was crying on her shoulder…literally.

A few moments later, Kate was still holding Amanda, but without raising her head, the girl said, "I fought with my mom about not taking ballet the night she died."

Kate's blood ran cold. *Oh, no.* She sat rigid, not wanting to say a word or move a muscle so that the girl would keep talking.

Was Amanda blaming herself for Joy's death?

"I told her I didn't want to dance, and she said she'd be really disappointed if I quit—because she had been a ballerina and had stopped dancing so she could have me and Calee. Since she couldn't dance anymore, she said we could make her happy by dancing for her."

Kate hated herself for what she was thinking—that she'd finally found the crack in Saint Joy's halo. Something that made this superhuman woman a bit more human. But it was nothing to celebrate, and she couldn't figure out why discovering Joy's flaw gave her such a sense of relief. Still, this wasn't about her or Joy right now. This girl was hurting.

"Before my mom and I could make up, she had to get something from the store. She said we'd talk about it later, after she got back. But she never came back."

Now Amanda's sobbing included great convulsions. Kate hugged her tighter.

"Sweetie, she was in an accident. It wasn't your fault. It certainly wasn't because you said you didn't want to dance anymore. You have to believe that. She wouldn't want you to be miserable."

"But she said my dancing made her happy. Everyone says she's in heaven now. And I think, if she is up there looking down on me, she will see me dancing. Even if I'm not any good at it, she'll be happy."

Kate held the girl and let her sob until she'd cried herself out. The teenage years were hard enough with the hormones and mean-girl battles. Navigating its rocky terrain without a mother's guidance made it particularly cruel.

"I met your mom once, and she was such a wonderful woman. I just have the strongest feeling that the only way she would be happy was to know that you were happy. In fact, I'll bet she'd be sad if she knew you were doing it for her and it was causing you so much pain."

The girl sat up and sniffed, swiping at fresh tears falling from her eyes. "Do you really think so?"

Kate had no idea. All she knew was that perfect Joy was not the perfect saint Kate had canonized Joy to be. She was human, pushing her daughters to live her unrequited dream. Who knows how long that would've lasted?

If Joy had made it home from the store that night,

maybe she would've returned with a new perspective and realized she couldn't force someone into an art they weren't born to do.

Since Kate was free to write her own ending to this story, she decided that Joy would've gotten it sooner rather than later.

"I really think so," Kate said. "I think you need to talk to your dad and be honest with him. But you know, right now, I'm dying of thirst. Would you come with me up to the house and have a glass of lemonade with me? You could wash your face and then help out with Kids' Day. Maybe your dad would let you stay afterward and ride for a while. We do have to call him and let him know you're safe. But maybe not just yet."

Chapter Fifteen

When Kate's call came in just after noon, Liam knew he had two choices: completely lose it or completely remain calm.

Thank God he'd had the presence of mind to choose the latter in the face of learning that his daughter had chosen to disobey him and walk down the highway to Macintyre Ranch. Good thing. Amanda's behavior problems weren't Kate's fault, and she'd called to tell him of his daughter's whereabouts.

Why hadn't someone from the dance studio called when they had realized Amanda wasn't in attendance? Given her absence this close to the end-of-the-year show and how the studio had declared any no-shows to be a federal offense, he thought they would've contacted him when Amanda didn't report for rehearsal.

The last person he'd expected to hear from was Kate. As much as he hated to admit it, it was the sound of her voice that had calmed him. He'd been caught off guard for the first few seconds of the call, but that had settled into an instant calm that buffered the anger that simmered over Amanda's blatant defiance.

How could his daughter do this? Put herself in danger, shirk her responsibility and make him look like a complete idiot when it came to parenting. Never more than now had he felt like an utter failure as a father.

"I'll be there to pick her up in fifteen minutes," he said. "If she's keeping you from doing something you need to do, just make her sit in a chair. I'm leaving now."

He'd given Calee the master bedroom since she couldn't navigate the stairs because of her sprain. He looked in to tell her that he was leaving for a few minutes, but she was sacked out. Probably from the painkillers. He would text her since, when she wasn't dancing, her phone was glued to her hand. She would be all right for the time it took for him to go out to Kate's and pick up Amanda. He'd need some time to think about a fitting punishment for Amanda.

"Liam, I don't mean to butt in, but when you get here, please be gentle with her," Kate said. "I think there's more going on here than simple teenage rebellion."

The care in Kate's voice touched Liam. He wasn't quite sure what to say to that or how to feel. He always wanted to be sensitive when it came to the girls, but after Kimela's manipulation, he wasn't keen on trusting anyone when it came to matters involving his family.

"Amanda is in big trouble," he said. "She skipped a rehearsal today. She walked along the highway alone. She went somewhere she wasn't supposed to be. She's never supposed to do that. She knows all of those things are cause for instant grounding. Kate, I really wish you would've never invited her to come over and ride. At least not without asking me first."

There was a long pause on the line. "I see," Kate finally said, her voice cold. "Well, just so we're clear, I didn't issue a specific invitation. It was more of an attempt at making conversation while I was staying with your daughter so that you could be at the hospital with Calee. I didn't mind helping you, but what I do resent is you somehow making me the bad guy in this, Liam."

Her words were a well-landed punch, and then the line went dead. Liam stood there staring at the phone, feeling duly put in his place.

Before Kate called Liam, she had intended to have Amanda ready to go so that she and Liam would only have to spend as little time as possible together. But after the way he'd talked to her—implying that somehow his daughter's running away from her dance class was Kate's fault—she'd be damned if she stood by again and let him get away with blaming her, when he was the one who needed to learn how to listen.

True, Amanda shouldn't have broken the rules, but Kate had heard loud and clear why the girl had done it. Not that it justified what she'd done, but Liam needed to know how important it was to talk things out with Amanda and to listen before he decided to dole out harsh punishments.

Kate had only met the girl twice. Yet Amanda was spilling her guts about important things that any parent should want to know were going on in his child's mind. And yes, Kate may have only met the girl two times, but Kate sensed that Amanda was a good kid at heart. A good kid who had known too much loss in too few years.

Kate had been fifteen years old when her own mother

had died. She understood what it was like to carry the burden of a mother's secrets. Here Amanda had been saddled with the weight of living out her mother's unrequited dream, a dream that not only wasn't her own, but was something she didn't even enjoy.

Since Liam had no qualms about making judgments against Kate, she fully intended to let Amanda stay busy with the Kids' Day events while Kate told him that if he was any kind of father, he'd listen to his daughter before he formed hurtful conclusions.

She was waiting for Liam outside on the office porch when he arrived.

"Hi." He bit off a stiff greeting. "Where is she?"

"She's occupied for the moment helping out with some special-needs kids we have in the barn today. She's really good at it. She's very sweet with the kids. I wanted you to see her in action before you labeled her, then jerked her out of here by her ear."

Liam frowned. "I would never lay a hand on my daughter in anger."

"I know that, Liam." She hoped her tone conveyed the depth of her annoyance. "It was a figure of speech."

He crossed his arms as if he were trying to block her out.

She softened her tone. "Listen, I know what Kimela Herring did. I know how she tried to use your girls to get to you and then planned to ship them off to New York. And I'm sorry about that. It wasn't right, and I know it must've been the last thing that you and the girls needed on top of everything else you were going through. I am not Kimela, and I am not trying to worm my way into your life, and especially not trying to come between you and your girls, but there is something you need to listen to. You said the thing about Kimela was that she didn't hear you. I hear you loud and clear. I know you don't want a relationship with me and that's fine, but if you jump on Amanda right now, you might not get a chance to *hear* something very important that she needs to say."

His anger evaporated, leaving only confusion and concern. He looked utterly exhausted standing there with the early afternoon sun casting shadows as it beat down on top of them. "What is it? What's wrong?"

His voice faltered, and for some insane reason that defied explanation, she wanted to put her arms around him and comfort him, but she knew that was the last thing that she should even be thinking right now.

Since she had his attention, she made a special effort to keep her voice soft. "I can't tell you, Liam. You and Amanda need to talk. Just please ask her *why* she doesn't want to go to dance class."

Now the confusion morphed to a shade of panic. "Is she *okay?*"

"She's not in physical danger but maybe some emotional turmoil. Just please be kind to her. She's a good kid, and I know she's sorry for not doing what you expected of her."

A flicker of apprehension played across his face.

"Come with me," she said. "I want to show you something."

She led him to the barn, and he followed without question. They stopped at the door. Amanda was working with a young boy with Down syndrome, helping him milk a cow. Amanda laughed and the boy squealed with delight as a stream of milk shot off to the side.

"That's okay, Brian," Amanda said. "You're doing a great job. Keep up the good work."

"'Manda, I love you." The boy got up off the stool and

threw his arms around his champion. When she hugged him back, she turned her head to the right and saw her dad standing there. Her face froze with apparent fear.

On Sunday Joy's mom, Judy, arrived for a visit and to help out with Calee. Judy and her husband, Walt, lived in Florida and were great about keeping in touch with Liam and the girls since Joy's death. After the funeral, swallowed by her grief, Judy had pulled Liam aside and told him, "You will always be my son. This doesn't change anything."

What would he do without Judy and Walt? They had been the family he'd never had growing up—instantly accepting him when he and Joy had started dating at such a ridiculously young age. They had been just a year older than his own girls when they'd met and fallen in love.

Despite how well his relationship with Joy had turned out, Liam wasn't sure if he would be so keen on one of his girls bringing home a boy right now and proclaiming they were in love.

These were different times, he told himself as he let himself into the kitchen through the garage door. It was 6:45 p.m. Judy was sitting at the kitchen table thumbing through a magazine and drinking a glass of what had to be her famous iced mint tea. She looked up and smiled when he walked in.

"Hi, hon. Did you have a nice day?"

The sight of her warmed his soul and reminded him that, other than his memories, Judy, Walt and the girls were the last vestiges he had of Joy.

"I had a good day," he said. "How about you?"

"It was nice and relaxing," she said. "I got to spend

some good time with the girls this morning before I took them to school."

Another nice thing about Judy's visits was that she always delighted in taking care of the girls. It gave him a much-needed break and Judy loved the time with her granddaughters. It was like a minivacation for everyone. Especially after what had happened between Amanda and him.

Things were fine, thanks to Kate.

Truth be told, Kate had been on his mind since Saturday when he'd gone over to pick up Amanda. Kate had stopped him from making a tactical error—a potentially devastating one as a parent that could've caused a cavernous divide between Amanda and him. All Kate had said was "You need to listen to her, Liam."

Amanda's punishment—if you could call it that—was to spend time volunteering for the once-a-month Kids' Day program and help in the office to plan events for it. Even though it was community service, he suspected it wasn't unbearable. And that was okay.

Thanks to Kate, instead of damaging his relationship with Amanda after the big blowup, he and his daughter were closer than ever; but still, it was nice to be able to give Amanda a little supervised distance.

"I hope you don't mind," Judy said. "But I sent Rosie home early."

"Not at all," Liam said. "She probably welcomed the break."

She nodded. "Would you like a glass of tea?"

There was something in her expression that said she wanted to talk. "Thank you," he said. "That sounds good."

The girls were at dance. Well, Amanda was dancing. She had to finish out the season, but she and Liam had agreed that she didn't have to go back once she was done. Calee was there in her wheelchair—a compromise.

Judy set the tea on the table and motioned for him to sit down. "So, tell me. Who is this Kate I've been hearing so much about?"

Liam couldn't understand it, but he felt as if he'd been caught. Judy's voice wasn't accusing, and she didn't seem upset. Still, Liam was taken aback.

"What do you mean?" he asked.

"All Amanda could talk about was this Kate, and I'm curious to know a little more about someone who seems to have captivated her so."

Judy had a twinkle in her blue eyes. She was a pretty woman with her gray hair, a little on the heavyset side.

After a moment of internal hemming and hawing, Liam finally said, "She heads up the foundation that's been raising money for the hospital's new pediatric surgical wing. She's become a good family friend." What he didn't say was *It's because of Kate that I learned that my own daughter hates dance. It's because of Kate that I realized I needed to listen more and judge less. It's because of Kate that I've learned that I just might be able to feel again....* But he couldn't say all that. Not to Joy's mother.

That would be the ultimate betrayal.

"Are you interested in Kate as more than a friend? Amanda certainly seems to love her."

The question made Liam flinch. He hoped that Judy hadn't noticed. God, sometimes he was so transparent.

"Amanda likes her because she has horses," Liam said. "Did she also tell you that she's probably not going to continue with dance after this season is over?"

"She did mention that," Judy said. "She says she

wants to volunteer for this Kids' Day outfit. She says Kate runs that, too. Sounds like a worthy way to spend her time."

Liam nodded.

"It also sounds like this Kate is a pretty nice person. When can I meet her?"

Liam froze. "I don't know about that."

What he really wanted to say was, if circumstances were different, he'd not only admit he was interested in Kate, he just might admit he'd developed feelings for her. But he had his hands full with work and caring for the girls. From what part of his life could he pull the time to nurture a relationship? It wouldn't be fair to anyone. So what was the point?

Besides, if circumstances were truly different, that would mean Joy would still be alive.

His heart was at war with his head, but his head had to rule. "The girls come first, Judy. I owe it to them to be here for them, at least until they are in college."

"Well, in some respects, that's a very short time because high school will go by in the blink of an eye. But the other side of the coin is that's five years of your life, and you and I both know, better than most, that tomorrow isn't guaranteed. You can't take a single day for granted."

"I know that. That's why I'm going to dedicate that time to Calee and Amanda."

Judy leaned in. "Honey, I don't think you understand what I'm saying—but, wait. Let me ask you something. Did you and Joy have a happy marriage?"

"Of course we did," he said. "I loved your daughter deeply. Still do."

"I know you do. And it won't mean you love her any less when you fall in love with someone else. In fact, it seems to me that the best tribute that you could pay her and your marriage will be if you want to get married again. A widower who is eager to get married again is paying his late wife the highest compliment, because that means he associates marriage with happiness. If he shies away from marriage, it's as if he's saying, 'Whoa, Nelly! I narrowly escaped that dungeon. I ain't going back there ever again.'

"You need to know that Walt and I will always love you, and we will always be part of your and the girls' lives. That will never end. Not even when you decide you're ready to pick up the pieces and move on with your life."

The air between them was heavy. For a moment Liam couldn't breathe for fear of falling apart. The emotion wasn't triggered by the sadness or reopened wounds. It came from a place much deeper. For the first time since he'd lost Joy, he saw the possibility ahead of him. He just might be able to love again.

It felt like he was being reborn, all at once learning how to walk and talk and feel once more. It was completely overwhelming. In the swirling maelstrom, he realized the only way to find his equilibrium was to listen…to his heart.

Chapter Sixteen

Kate arrived at Laurel Grove Park ten minutes early. Liam had called her that morning and asked if they could meet there for lunch. He wanted to talk to her. Out of self-preservation, she'd declined. But when he'd persisted, she'd relented.

As she stood under the weeping willow tree waiting for him, she was as nervous as if this were a real date. But it wasn't, she reminded herself, and she did her best to ignore the disappointment that lay leaden and betraying beneath her breastbone.

She had an inkling this urgent meeting might have to do with Amanda. Kate had agreed to let the girl—who had proven to be quite good with the Kids' Day children—serve as a regular volunteer at the ranch over the summer. In fact, if she still proved as passionate about helping out after next month's event, Kate planned to surprise Amanda by bringing her on as a paid part-time employee. But Kate would cross that bridge when she came to it. Right now she had to get hold of the nerves turning her belly upside down.

As she waited, she watched a pair of little girls playing on the jungle gym inside a fenced-in playground. Two moms with babies in strollers talked as the preschool-aged girls sped down the deep green slide and then ran around the area before they made their final approach to the swings. When they got there, one of them waved at Kate. The sweet gesture made Kate's heart squeeze as she waved back.

Instinctively her hand landed on her flat belly. For an almost imperceptible second, what was left of the once well-constructed fire wall that had formerly surrounded Kate's heart tumbled.

The little girls looked like they were about four years old. The same age Kate's baby would've been if the child had lived. Kate's gaze zipped back to the mothers, sitting on the wooden park bench in their capri pants, colorful blouses and casual sandals; it was a sharp contrast to the business suit and pumps that Kate wore. The women talked and laughed as if they didn't have a care in the world.

Kate realized that things weren't always as they seemed on the surface; despite having healthy children, the women probably weren't strife-free. Nobody was; people hid their cares and worries behind smiles and jokes and jobs that kept them so busy they didn't have time to dwell on how life had shortchanged them...or how they'd shortchanged themselves. Kate knew this trick. She'd become an expert at the masquerade.

Standing here in her buttoned-up business suit with her guard down, she let herself wonder for the first time since the miscarriage how having a baby might have changed her life. What if she'd gone through with the wedding and had married Gibson Baker, even though she didn't love him the way he deserved to be loved?

Would she have learned to be happy with a man she didn't love? Would they have tried again and again until they'd eventually had the children Kate had so desperately wanted? Would she have grown to love Gibson simply because he was the father of her children? Or, like her mother, would Kate have lived a restless life making miserable the man who loved her? Would she have driven him to the bottle the same way her mother had driven her father over the edge?

Kate loved Liam. She just didn't want to be on the opposite side of that futile love equation, either. Not when his heart would always belong to another woman. Loving this emotionally unavailable man had reduced her to settling for pathetic stolen kisses and contrived dates.

Tears stung her eyes. She wasn't going to do this.

Not here. Not now. She needed to leave while she could.

She turned to walk away and almost bumped head-on into Liam.

"Are you okay?" he asked.

"Sure, I have something in my shoe." She bent down and removed her pump, shook out the imaginary pebble, blinking away the moisture in her eyes.

She had to get a hold of herself before meeting this man. It had been a long time since she'd let her guard down so that anything like the sight of little girls playing on a playground could reduce her to tears. Meeting him here was a bad idea.

But before she could stand up straight, Liam's hand was on her elbow steadying her. His touch nearly seared her arm. He smiled at her, and she wasn't sure if his smile was apologetic or seductive…but that's what she got for playing with fire.

She finally had the fortitude to jerk free from his grasp.

"Kate?" he said.

"I need to go, Liam," she said. "I can't do this again."

She started to walk away, but he grabbed her hand.

"Please wait," he said. "That's what I wanted to talk to you about."

She shook her head. "Please don't. I heard you the first time when you said you didn't want to get involved until after the girls were grown. I'm not Kimela. I get it. I thought we covered this when you came to pick up Amanda last week."

"You and Kimela are polar opposites. So let's not even go there, okay? And, yes, we did cover this last week…or at least part of it. But things are different now."

His voice was steady and kind. She didn't know if he was baiting her the same way he had the night of their big date—reeling her in with smooth double-talk, only to throw her back after she bit.

"Liam, I know what it's like to be in an unbalanced relationship. Where someone loves you, but you can't return the feelings. It stinks almost as much as it does to be the one who loves more. I care about you, but I can't let myself fall in love with a man who will always be in love with someone else."

"Could you learn to love a man who is willing to love you enough for both of you? Because I love you, Kate. Before I met you, I thought I'd never be able to love again, but you've shown me that's not true. You've saved me. I'm willing to wait as long as it takes for you to love and trust me."

Kate stood there, stunned, not sure she'd heard him right, but the look on his face assured her that she had.

"Kate, I don't want another day to go by without you in my life. We can take things slowly, but please say you'll give us a chance."

"What about the girls?" Kate asked, still afraid to let down her newly constructed guard. Yet she felt it slipping away, like a person who was hanging on to the ledge of a skyscraper by their fingertips.

"Amanda loves you," he said. "In fact, I think if she had to choose between you and me, she'd choose you. Calee loves everyone. No offense to you. I guess I should say Calee loves dance. She's just an all-around happy kid as long as she's dancing. And I loved you from the moment you first tried to talk me into doing that crazy auction. I'm so glad you did. I hope you haven't given up on me."

She answered him with a kiss that conveyed every word her heart wanted to say, but her brain couldn't form. And he held her like he was afraid to let her go.

Then she remembered there were children nearby, and she pulled away. "I love you, Liam. Always have. Always will."

Ten days later, Liam and Kate were dancing at the Doctor's Ball in the Chantilly Ballroom at the Dallas Hilton Anatole.

"I'm the luckiest man in Texas," Liam whispered in her ear as they swayed together under a sea of blue-and-white ambient lighting to the strains of a full orchestra playing "Unforgettable."

The ball was an annual event hosted by Celebration Memorial Hospital's Department of Charitable Giving.

All proceeds from this dinner dance would benefit the new pediatric surgical wing.

Traditionally the Doctor's Ball raised in excess of one hundred thousand dollars each year. This year everyone was particularly excited because it was sure to bring in the last of the funds needed for this project, which had united the entire community of Celebration, Texas.

It helped, too, that the current honorary chairman was none other than Hugh Newman, who happened to be Hollywood's hottest leading man and *People* magazine's reigning Sexiest Man Alive.

Even with Hugh in attendance, the fact that Kate seemed to only have eyes for Liam just made him love her more.

"Well, if it isn't the Ten-Thousand-Dollar Man," said Cullen Dunlevy. He was dancing with Maya LeBlanc and steered her over next to Liam. "I see we didn't have to force you to come to this fund-raiser. Looks like the bachelor auction turned out better than you thought it would."

Cullen winked at Kate.

"I'll concede," said Liam. "You're right. What I thought was going to be a miserable experience turned out to be one of the best things that's happened to me in a very long time. But isn't it interesting that you and our colleagues—Vogler, Roberts, Chamberlin, Benton and Lennox—were the ones who were so gung ho on the bachelor auction and yet all came stag to the ball tonight."

Cullen laughed. "We may not have gotten as lucky as you and Kate, but at least we're out there trying."

"Lucky me, I am off the market." He leaned in and planted a kiss on Kate's delicious lips.

"And I am the one who called this relationship before I even met you, Liam. Did I not, *ma cheri?*" Maya arched her right eyebrow and waited expectantly for Kate to give her her due.

"Yes, you did, Maya," said Kate. "You are a sage woman. I will happily endorse your matchmaking skills."

"You two silly lovers," she said. "You wasted all this time fighting fate. Had you just listened to me, you could've saved yourselves a world of heartache. But *non.* And you are not the only ones who do not listen. Those two over there—" she nodded discreetly toward Hugh Newman and Bia Anderson, the editor of the *Dallas Journal of Business and Development* "—they have been canoodling all evening. Even though they seem cozy, they are not destined to end up together."

She pursed her lips and gave a single shoulder shrug.

"Did you tell them that?" Kate asked, sounding a little stunned.

"Mais, oui." Maya sighed. "But they do not listen."

"Maya, I don't mean to be rude," Kate said. "But do you know Bia well enough to give her unsolicited relationship advice? I don't mean to hurt your feelings, but that was part of the problem when you told me Liam was my soul mate."

"She told you we were soul mates?" Liam asked.

Kate nodded. "Yes, about five minutes into our first face-to-face conversation."

Maya laughed, but there was a sad note to the sound. "I know Bia better than anyone realizes, and I will be here for her when her heart is broken."

"That's so sad," Kate said. "Especially when I want everyone to be as deliriously happy as we are."

"Oh, no worries, *ma cheri,*" she said. "She has already met her perfect match. She just doesn't know it yet."

Cullen hummed the *Twilight Zone* music and they all laughed.

"Even you, Dr. Dunlevy. You, too, will meet your soul mate one of these days."

"But I'm dancing with her now." He twirled Maya away from him and then spun her back into his chest.

"You are a handsome, charming man," she said. "Alas, I am not the one for you."

"And how do you know these things, Maya?" Liam asked.

Maya smiled and shook her head. "It is just an intuition. I know that they are wrong for each other—" she nodded again to Bia and Hugh "—the same way I knew that the two of you will have a long, happy life together. That's why I am the matchmaker. And that is why I was willing to bet ten thousand dollars that you were right for each other."

"What?" Liam asked.

Kate's eyes widened. "Were *you* the one who sent the anonymous ten-thousand-dollar check to the Macintyre Foundation?"

Maya simply smiled as she gave her adorable one-shoulder shrug, then spun away from Cullen, who followed her into the middle of the crowded dance floor.

"So Maya was our benefactor," said Kate.

"I'd say she bet right on the money." Liam pulled Kate close. "But we are definitely the winners. I love you, Kate."

"I love you, too," Kate said. "Like I've never loved anyone before."

* * * * *

COMING NEXT MONTH FROM

H HARLEQUIN®

SPECIAL EDITION

Available February 18, 2014

#2317 LASSOED BY FORTUNE
The Fortunes of Texas: Welcome to Horseback Hollow
by Marie Ferrarella

Liam Jones doesn't want any part of newfound Fortune relatives—or the changes they bring to Horseback Hollow. *He's crazy,* thinks Julia Tierney. The ambitious beauty was always the one Liam could never snag in high school. When Julia becomes the chef at a local restaurant, Julia and Liam find that old attractions die hard....

#2318 THE DADDY SECRET
Return to Brighton Valley • by Judy Duarte

When Mallory Dickinson gave up her son, she never thought she'd see Brighton Valley—or her baby's father, Rick Martinez—again. A decade later, she's back in town with her son, whom she adopted—and Rick's become a responsible veterinarian. Can the former bad boy and the social worker let their guards down to allow love in?

#2319 A PROPOSAL AT THE WEDDING
Bride Mountain • by Gina Wilkins

Father-of-the-bride Paul Brennan can't help but find himself tempted by irresistible innkeeper Bonnie Carmichael. Trouble arises, though, since Bonnie hopes to create a life and family at Bride Mountain Inn, and Paul's already done fatherhood. In the shadow of Bride Mountain, love blooms as they find their way to a happily-ever-after.

#2320 FINDING FAMILY...AND FOREVER?
The Bachelors of Blackwater Lake • by Teresa Southwick

Kidnapped as a child, Emma Robbins heads to Blackwater Lake to find her birth family. In the process, she becomes the nanny to Dr. Justin Flint's young son. The handsome widower is unwillingly attracted to the lovely newcomer, who loves the boy as her own, but secrets and lies may undermine the family they begin to build.

#2321 HER ACCIDENTAL ENGAGEMENT • by Michelle Major

Single mom Julia Morgan needs a man—not for love, but to keep custody of her son, Charlie. Local police chief Sam Callahan wants to keep his family out of his love life. The two engage in a romance of convenience, but what begins as a pretense might just evolve into true love.

#2322 THE ONE HE'S BEEN LOOKING FOR • by Joanna Sims

World-renowned photographer Ian Sterling is going blind, and he wants to find the model of his dreams before he loses his sight entirely. He finds his muse in rebellious Jordan Brand, but there's more than a camera between these two. To truly heal, Ian must open his heart to see what's been in front of him all along.

YOU CAN FIND MORE INFORMATION ON UPCOMING HARLEQUIN® TITLES, FREE EXCERPTS AND MORE AT WWW.HARLEQUIN.COM.

HSECNM0214

REQUEST YOUR FREE BOOKS!
2 FREE NOVELS PLUS 2 FREE GIFTS!

⊕ HARLEQUIN®

SPECIAL EDITION
Life, Love & Family

YES! Please send me 2 FREE Harlequin® Special Edition novels and my 2 FREE gifts (gifts are worth about $10). After receiving them, if I don't wish to receive any more books, I can return the shipping statement marked "cancel." If I don't cancel, I will receive 6 brand-new novels every month and be billed just $4.74 per book in the U.S. or $5.24 per book in Canada. That's a savings of at least 14% off the cover price! It's quite a bargain! Shipping and handling is just 50¢ per book in the U.S. and 75¢ per book in Canada.* I understand that accepting the 2 free books and gifts places me under no obligation to buy anything. I can always return a shipment and cancel at any time. Even if I never buy another book, the two free books and gifts are mine to keep forever.

235/335 HDN F45Y

Name	(PLEASE PRINT)	
Address		Apt. #
City	State/Prov.	Zip/Postal Code

Signature (if under 18, a parent or guardian must sign)

Mail to the **Harlequin® Reader Service:**
IN U.S.A.: P.O. Box 1867, Buffalo, NY 14240-1867
IN CANADA: P.O. Box 609, Fort Erie, Ontario L2A 5X3

Want to try two free books from another line?
Call 1-800-873-8635 or visit www.ReaderService.com.

* Terms and prices subject to change without notice. Prices do not include applicable taxes. Sales tax applicable in N.Y. Canadian residents will be charged applicable taxes. Offer not valid in Quebec. This offer is limited to one order per household. Not valid for current subscribers to Harlequin Special Edition books. All orders subject to credit approval. Credit or debit balances in a customer's account(s) may be offset by any other outstanding balance owed by or to the customer. Please allow 4 to 6 weeks for delivery. Offer available while quantities last.

Your Privacy—The Harlequin® Reader Service is committed to protecting your privacy. Our Privacy Policy is available online at www.ReaderService.com or upon request from the Harlequin Reader Service.

We make a portion of our mailing list available to reputable third parties that offer products we believe may interest you. If you prefer that we not exchange your name with third parties, or if you wish to clarify or modify your communication preferences, please visit us at www.ReaderService.com/consumerschoice or write to us at Harlequin Reader Service Preference Service, P.O. Box 9062, Buffalo, NY 14269. Include your complete name and address.

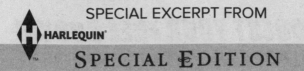
When Mallory Dickinson is reunited with her first love, she has to decide whether to tell him her deepest secret—that her young son is his biological child!

***

Mallory took a deep breath, probably trying to gather her thoughts—or maybe to lie.

But it didn't take a brain surgeon to see the truth. She'd kept the baby she was supposed to have given up for adoption, and she'd let ten years go by without telling Rick.

Betrayal gnawed at his gut.

"Lucas called you a doctor," she said, arching a delicate brow.

"I'm a veterinarian. My clinic is just down the street."

As she mulled that over, Lucas sidled up to Rick wearing a bright-eyed grin. "Did you come to ask my mom about Buddy?"

No, the dog was the last thing he'd come to talk to Mallory about. And while he hadn't been sure just how the conversation was going to unfold when he arrived, it had just taken a sudden and unexpected turn.

"Why would he come to talk to me about his dog?" Mallory asked her son.

Or rather *their* son. Who else could the boy be?

Lucas, who wore a smile that indicated he was completely oblivious to the tension building between the adults, approached Mallory. "Because Buddy needs a home. Since we have a yard now, can I have him? *Please?* I promise to take care of him and walk him and everything."

She said, "We'll talk about it later."

"Okay. Thanks." He flashed Rick a smile, then turned and headed toward the stairs.

As Lucas was leaving, Rick's gaze traveled from the boy to Mallory and back again. Finally, when they were alone, Rick folded his arms across his chest, shifted his weight to one hip and smirked.

"Cute kid," he said.

Mallory flushed brighter still, and she wiped her palms along her hips.

Nervous, huh? Rick's internal B.S. detector slipped into overdrive.

Well, she ought to be.

When Rick had found out about her pregnancy, he'd been only seventeen, but he'd offered to quit school, get a job and marry her. However, her grandparents had decided that she was too young and convinced her that adoption was the only way to go. So they'd sent her to Boston to live with her aunt Carrie until the birth.

Yet in spite of what she'd promised him when she left, she hadn't come back to Brighton Valley. And within six months' time, he'd lost all contact with her—through no fault of his own.

Apparently, she'd had a change of heart about the adoption. And about the feelings she'd claimed she'd had for him, too.

***

Enjoy this sneak peek from USA TODAY *bestselling author Judy Duarte's THE DADDY SECRET, the first book in* RETURN TO BRIGHTON VALLEY, *a brand-new miniseries coming in March 2014!*

Copyright © 2014 by Judy Duarte

HARLEQUIN®

SPECIAL EDITION

Life, Love and Family

First comes the wedding...then love?

Don't miss
HER ACCIDENTAL ENGAGEMENT
by Michelle Major

Single mom Julia Morgan needs a man—not for
love, but to keep custody of her son, Charlie.
Local police chief Sam Callahan wants to keep
his family out of his love life. The two engage in
a romance of convenience, but what begins as a
pretense might just evolve into true love.

*Look for HER ACCIDENTAL ENGAGEMENT
next month from Harlequin® Special Edition®
wherever books and ebooks are sold!*

www.Harlequin.com

HSE65803